# BETWEEN HOME & HEARTBREAK

## GAMBLING HEARTS SERIES

JACQUI NELSON

Cover design by The Killion Group, Inc

ISBN ebook: 978-0-9936387-5-6
ISBN print: 978-0-9936387-4-9

PRAISE FOR THE GAMBLING HEARTS SERIES...

*Between Love & Lies* - **Book 1**

"I loved the twists and turns this book takes. If you want a top-shelf historical western romance, you won't go wrong with this." ~ Linda Broday (New York Times & USA Today bestselling author of historical western romance)

"I couldn't read it fast enough and I didn't want it to end either." ~ Bob

"The chemistry in this book sizzles from the very first pages. The characters come to life with vibrant color and intensity." ~ Heather C.

"Held me in its grasp and wouldn't let me go until the oh-so-satisfying conclusion." ~ Diane B.

*Between Home & Heartbreak* - **Book 2**

"A western romance, thrill ride, filled with twists and turns in every chapter!" ~ A.P.Reader

"A fun, yet nail biting story." ~ Christine W.

"Open the book and get swept away!" ~ Little Piggy's

"Kept my attention until the end! I just loved her heroine Eldorado Jane" ~ Nicole L.

## DEDICATION

To all my readers whose friendships (and critiques, beta reads, plot brainstorming, reviews, and positive energy) helped me finish this book, including...

Nora, Marjorie, Marion Ann, Jo-Ann C, and Jacquie B (who stuck with me since my first book)

Liette B and Tina H (who jumped on-board during the pre-release of book 1 in my series, and who loved book 2 as much as the first)

And to everyone who has ever searched for a place called home...

For me, home is more than a place, more than four walls and a roof to keep me warm and safe. *El Dorado* was a mythical place of allegedly unimaginable riches. In Spanish, *El Dorado* translates to "the gilded one," which seemed a fitting title for a Wild West show superstar. So Eldorado Jane was born, and the theme of searching for home came into the title *Between Home & Heartbreak*.

Eldorado Jane's story and Lewis' (whom I introduced in *Between Love & Lies*, book 1 in my *Gambling Hearts* series) is for everyone who has ever searched for a place called home or *El Dorado*, which instead of a place might be a person giving the greatest gold of all—love and unwavering friendship.

# ELDORADO
~ By Edgar Allan Poe ~

Gaily bedight,
A gallant knight,
In sunshine and in shadow,
Had journeyed long,
Singing a song,
In search of Eldorado.

But he grew old—
This knight so bold—
And o'er his heart a shadow
Fell as he found
No spot of ground
That looked like Eldorado.

And, as his strength
Failed him at length,
He met a pilgrim shadow—
"Shadow," said he,
"Where can it be—
This land of Eldorado?"

"Over the Mountains
Of the Moon,
Down the Valley of the Shadow,
Ride, boldly ride,"
The shade replied—
"If you seek for Eldorado!"

# PROLOGUE

*Outside Juniper Flats, Texas*
*Spring, 1861*

Lewis struggled to stay upright—and not hit the ground like some pretender grasping for a fool's gold. Kneeling on his galloping pony, he clutched the saddle horn and stuck his other arm straight out for balance. Tonight he'd succeed. He'd prove his worth.

He'd keep up with his best friend, the invincible Jane Dority.

Beside him, easily holding the same pose on her horse Scout, Jane called to him, "Forget your father. Focus on me. They say the best partners act in harmony."

"Who says?"

"The owner of *Gypson's Medicine Show*."

Gypson also claimed his elixir cured every illness and strengthened the sensational acts that alternated between his sales pitches. Lewis' father said practice and perseverance, not doctored-up whiskey, made good performances. But Jane had talked incessantly about Gypson and his horse-riding acrobat after watching them captivate Juniper Flats' cheering townsfolk an hour ago.

Trying to duplicate one of their maneuvers while racing through a twilight field with storm clouds thickening overhead made him suddenly wish he'd never come to town. "Everyone's obsessed with that show."

"You're the same with roundup. Have been for years."

He lowered his chin against the rain that began falling and Jane's perceptiveness.

"Bet your father takes you next year." Her words came quick, with conviction.

"You said that last year." And the year before. And still his father kept saying he was too young, especially with the ongoing range disputes. But this year, his father and Jane's had agreed to take their friend Noah, who was also eleven and had been the same height as Lewis—until this spring.

"One day you'll tower over me. Bet you're as tall as Noah next year."

"Get out of my head, Jane!" He huffed out a breath, trying to expel the expectations—his and everyone else's— that pestered him like a saddle cinched too tight.

"Partners should embrace connections."

"Enough quoting Gypson," he grumbled. "Just teach me to ride like you." Then his father might see him differently and let him help bring in the strays from the high country.

"Next year you'll work with the men every day. And I..." Jane's voice wavered. "I won't be riding."

Lewis shook his head in disbelief and swayed precariously on Sergeant. He pressed his knees against the pommel and stared straight ahead, searching for a balance that was difficult to find. "You'll always ride."

"My mom needs help cooking for the Ballantyne hands.

No time for horses, she says. Next year you'll be a better rider than me."

Laughter burst from his lips. He'd never beat Jane on a horse. No one would. Not even the girl in the show they'd recently watched; the rider whose routine they now mimicked.

"I'll settle for being your equal at riding." That would impress his father. And that's all he wanted, tonight and tomorrow. *Hold on. Don't fall. Keep up with Jane.*

"Why should anyone settle?" Jane and Scout edged ahead.

He urged Sergeant to regain the lost ground. Jane kept pulling away. Sweat stung his eyes. Then the heavens opened up and washed away everything, including all sight of Jane.

"Come back!" Fear clawed up his spine until he glimpsed the tip of her long brown braid flying behind her. She'd slowed down for him. "Let's go home."

"I'm not ready." Despite her curt reply, Jane continued slowing Scout until her entire silhouette was visible.

The tightness squeezing his chest eased. Only to return with a vengeance when she yelled, "I won't stop riding."

"It's raining too hard." The downpour pummeled his entire body, turning the saddle slick and slippery beneath him. "We have to stop!"

"The star of the show wouldn't let a little rain stop her."

Fear and frustration warred in his veins. "Stop pretending. You're no star. You're just plain Jane Dority!"

Her shoulders drooped and then snapped straight. He stiffened as well, with remorse. He'd finally said the name too many used. Despite being a dazzling rider, his friend was plain in every other way.

He'd let her down—with the worst words possible.

Thunder rumbled, chastising him, shaking him to the bone. He strained to stay on Sergeant and say something to dilute the sting of his foolishness.

Ahead, Jane's silhouette grew smaller, fainter. "Maybe I'll ride all night. All day tomorrow, too." She was leaving him again.

He couldn't let her ride into the night alone. A best friend deserved better.

He urged Sergeant to go faster. A chant built in his head along with the pounding of Sergeant's hooves. *Forget about falling. You can do this. You have to do this. Say you're sorry before you drive her away.*

"Jane—"

"No, I won't go home till I'm ready. Till I'm a star so bright, I'll blind you with my brilliance."

Lightning blazed, concealing Jane, Scout, and even Sergeant, still galloping valiantly beneath him. A heartbeat later came the roar.

The blast of light and noise enveloped him. His body flew from the saddle, his hands lost the horn, the reins—leaving him with only the air.

# CHAPTER 1

*18 years later...*
*High country above Juniper Flats*

*L*ying flat on his back, squinting at the sycamores swaying against a hazy blue sky, every bone in Lewis Adams' body ached, berating him for letting the half-broke Appaloosa Cayuse toss him out of the saddle and over the fence. The land he loved reverberated beneath him. He'd be tempted to stay here if he didn't have nine more prickly horses requiring his attention. Training them in time was all that mattered.

The silhouette of a woman, framed by a sunshine halo, leaned over him and cast a soothing shadow. "You almost had him." Her smooth-as-honey voice held a hint of amusement.

At last, an angel had descended from the heavens to ease his burdens. One bearing encouraging words as well as laughter. Exactly the kind he liked, and needed.

An easy smile lifted his lips. Now here was a reason for

lying in the dirt. Damned if he'd move and spook her. *Stay with me. Don't disappear.*

She leaned closer, revealing deep brown eyes rich as polished heartwood.

"Your eyes are—" His breath lodged in his chest, then found freedom with the word, "stunning."

Her eyebrows shot up in surprise. Then her laughter floated down around him like a warm embrace. "I think your fall, not my eyes, stunned you. Next time keep *your* eyes on your mount's ears. They'll tell you which way he plans to jump."

His grin grew. Horse sense, a kind heart, and a sharp wit. His angel and her mesmerizing eyes were a dream come true.

The clatter of hooves swelled above the earth's fading tremors. Recognition shook the fog from his brain. His visitor was one of the three riders he'd glimpsed approaching before he'd been bucked off. Her mount had thundered ahead like a towering black cloud and now hovered next to the corral, looking at his rainbow assortment of horses.

The woman standing over him was real.

Who was she? Why was she at the Dority homestead? No one came up here for months on end. Craving a better look at her, he tried to push up on his elbows.

"Lie still." Crouching on her heels, she laid her gloved hand on his shoulder. Even wrapped in soft kidskin, her light touch jolted him like a lightning bolt, then held him hostage. He'd do whatever she said as long as she kept touching him...and staring at him with her angel eyes.

"We must talk before they join us." Her voice had dropped to a conspiratorial whisper. "I'm sorry. I'm going to hurt you again."

"Eldora, is he dead?" The not-too-distant bellow made them both flinch. The eagerness in that shout rang in his skull like the bells of hell anticipating a funeral.

In one swift movement, Angel Eyes retreated to stand straight as a cedar, a stride away.

He reached out to stop her from going farther. Only the fact that she didn't, kept him on his backside. That and the twinge in his ribs. Was this what she'd meant about hurting him again?

She wasn't responsible for his fall.

"He'll live," she called over her shoulder, revealing a braid so long its yellow-as-a-meadowlark's-breast ribbon brushed her waist. "He simply had the wind knocked out of him." Her gaze went to the corral and the Appaloosa that'd done the deed, still snorting and stomping in displeasure. "You've more courage than compassion to ride that frightened animal before earning his trust."

The disappointment in her tone stung more than her words. But trust took time, and the Rangers would return in three weeks.

The approaching riders skidded to a halt beside her. So close they kicked up a cloud of dust and whipped the woman's skirt around her legs.

"Watch out!" He launched to his feet, ignoring the pain the sudden movement caused along with the spinning in his head.

Only the woman remained still, seeming oblivious to her companions' lack of skill or care for her safety. He kept moving, pulling her close, shielding her with his body. When he halted, his pain drew all of his attention, stabbing like a red hot poker and making him groan.

Wide-eyed with concern, she finally moved. Her firm grip on his elbow drew him even closer. Below him, the fine lines around her eyes crinkled as she contemplated him with warmth again. "I said you'd tower over me one day."

A frown tightened his brow. When had she said that? He'd never met her before.

"Eldora." The baritone boomed again, this time close and crackling with censure. Its owner, a barrel-chested man sporting a wealth of red hair turning white at the temples, stood next to the woman, his beefy paw on her shoulder.

Lewis' protective instinct flared again. "You could've trampled her. You're a piss-poor rider."

"I could ride circles around you, boy."

"Roy, be nice. He doesn't know you or what we do. Why not be grateful someone shows concern for my well-being, even when unnecessary?" Angel Eyes pushed away from both of them.

The loss of her touch left him adrift, awash with disappointment. His gaze clung to her as she retrieved the reins of the jet-black giant now cozying up to Lila, his faithful roan and his only saddle-broke horse, tethered outside the corral.

"I am concerned that you left my side and raced ahead." The newcomer's tone, more condescending than anything, made Lewis' hands twitch with the unusual urge to take him down a notch.

"You know..." The man paused, like a preacher embarking on an oft-used sermon, and added a scowl to his onslaught. "I dislike it when—"

"I break from our routine." She met the man's glare head-on. "Your number of dislikes has grown over the years."

"I would dislike it if you hurt yourself. My show depends on you."

"You used to call it our show."

*A show?* What show? The word cast a heavy pall over him. He'd only seen one show. The night he'd lost Jane. A night followed by days, then years of praying Jane would come home, until time smothered his hopes. Until today.

Could this woman be Jane?

He scanned her face, searching for his answer there. She shared Jane's plain features, and the lines framing her eyes and mouth made him guess her age close to his twenty-nine years. Jane was only one year younger.

"Have we met before?" The minute her gaze met his again, he knew they hadn't. He wouldn't forget those eyes.

But her long brown braid, now draped over her shoulder, was familiar. As was the way she stood and moved, graceful as a dancer, agile as a cat...in fitted, finely-stitched clothing that only came with high-priced city tailoring, clothing out of place on a remote country hillside.

Angel Eyes didn't belong anywhere near him, his dusty garments purchased at Juniper Flats' general store, and the land he'd finally made his—the Dority homestead with its one-room cabin and corrals hewn from the surrounding trees. She had money, while he'd spent his last dollar buying his new home and the corral full of unbroken—and even worse, half-broke and messed up in the process—horses.

"It's understandable if you don't remember me." Her silky-smooth voice caught on the word *me* before continuing. "It's been a long time."

"I don't know you." *I wish I did.* That was part of the problem. That, and the fact that he couldn't stop staring at her. But his frank appraisal had yet to bring even the hint of a blush to her cheeks.

Angel Eyes was used to being looked at, probably by every man in Texas. Jealousy, hard and swift, left him rigid.

She wasn't Jane, and she wasn't *his* angel. She had a name. One he'd avoided acknowledging.

He forced his body to relax and his mouth to move. "I don't know anyone named Eldora."

"When I was young, I had a different name." She stared at him, waiting.

What was she trying to tell him? Before the man she'd called Roy arrived, she'd said they needed to talk. She glanced at the man now, a hurried look through narrowed eyes. She was hiding something—from both of them.

"Introductions are in order." Her companion thrust out his hand, and Lewis took it. Firm grip, squeezed a little too hard. The man didn't let go.

Neither did Lewis.

"I'm Colonel Roy Calhoun." Pride oozed from the title. His name fit his clothing: a wide-brimmed hat worn at a cocky angle, high leather boots polished to an obsidian gleam, and a buckskin jacket with more fringe than was functional. He looked like he'd stepped out of a dime novel.

Calhoun gestured over his shoulder to a lean man wearing a federal blue suit. "Mr. Vandrill is my personal guard, my lawyer, and the top marksman in my show."

A leather strap slung diagonally across the man's chest held a rifle on his back, leaving his hands free to hold the reins of a pair of sleek mounts, one of which shone as white as the man's silver-blond hair.

"No one's better with a Winchester or Sharps rifle," Calhoun added.

Lewis shook his head in disbelief. Why would Calhoun need a lawyer or a guard, or even a sharpshooter, up here in the hill country? And why did he keep mentioning a show? Was everything he said part of an act?

"You a real Colonel, or did your title come with your show?"

Calhoun's grip on his hand tightened. "I am a West Point graduate. Received my first promotion at twenty-one in the Nebraska Territory fighting the Sioux. Fought countless battles since. And many wars, including the one between the States. I am always on the winning side. I make sure of it."

Lewis bit back his laugh. He'd met similar men before, men always needing to prove something, men not completely comfortable in their own skin—which for this one in particular appeared to be equal parts bear and peacock rolled into one.

He cast a pointed glance at Calhoun's hand still squeezing his.

Calhoun finally let go and swept his arm in a grand arc toward Eldora. "And this is Mrs. Calhoun, my wife and the star of my show."

*His wife?* The revelation hit him like a sucker punch to the jaw. It sent his head spinning again. She had to be fifteen, maybe even twenty, years younger than Calhoun. He didn't want her to be married to Calhoun or to anyone.

He buried his disappointment in a question. "This show, would it be Colonel Calhoun's Show?"

"Why, yes." Calhoun drew himself up like a rooster in a hen house. "*Colonel Calhoun's Wondrous West,* to be exact. I have assembled the finest acts and been invited to entertain in the highest circles. I knew even a rustic like you would have heard of me."

"I haven't. Just a lucky guess." When directed at him, Calhoun's condescending tone concerned him little. But his presence disturbed him a lot.

Why was he here? Where had he come from?

Definitely a place where you could find everything you desired, even if you'd never known you wanted it. Lewis hadn't traveled much, but he'd been to Dodge City and the string of colorful camp towns from here to there and back again. He'd never glimpsed anything or anyone as captivating as Eldora: a woman fully dressed, covered from chin to toe, wearing a jacket that hugged her like a lover's eager embrace...until it fell in a flare of ruffles over the back of her skirt, over the delectable curve of her—

He locked his attention on the uninspiring territory of Calhoun's equally well-tailored but fully unpleasant form. "You from San Antonio or Austin?"

"Neither, my boy!" Even though they were the same height, Calhoun managed to peer down his nose at him. "The entire country is our home. We tour everywhere. Last summer we entertained all of New York. Soon we shall journey to England and Europe."

Lewis released a slow whistle. "Next thing you'll be telling me is you received an invite from the Queen."

Calhoun's jaw tightened. "Only a matter of time."

"And you...Mrs. Calhoun?" Lewis' gaze swung back to Eldora like a compass needle seeking true north, while his mouth resisted calling her a missus. "What's your claim to fame in this Wonderful Show?"

Eldora's gaze narrowed. "You really don't remember me?"

He shook his head.

Calhoun huffed in displeasure. "You will once you learn that my wife is—"

"I'm a trick rider called Eldorado Jane."

The name made his gut clench. Why must she keep resurrecting memories of Jane? He'd give anything to see his

Jane again, but this sophisticated woman standing before him was as far from Jane Dority as the sun from the moon.

Her gaze narrowed even more.

When he realized he was scowling at her, he plastered a smile on his face, hoping it would conceal his frustration. "And you're here because...?"

Eldora fidgeted with the yellow ribbon at the end of her braid and remained silent.

Calhoun did not. "My wife is the Dority's long-lost daughter."

Lewis' smile vanished. So did the air in his lungs. "No. She's not."

Eldora straightened her shoulders, as if bracing for battle. "Those are some fine horses in your corral. Perhaps you will name a pair Sergeant and Scout?"

Surprise rocked Lewis. Anger followed fast and held him firm. "You talked to someone in town." She couldn't be Jane. He'd prove it. "Just because you know Ol' Sarge's name doesn't mean you're Jane."

Her gaze held his, direct and certain. "You never called him Sarge. You wouldn't let me either."

She was good at guessing as well. Either that, or she'd read the truth on his face. Unlike her, he was a poor liar and always had been. Seeking a diversion, he thrust his chin at her hulk of a horse, with a mane as long as Samson's. "What's that brute's name?"

"Samson."

Did she read minds and as well as faces?

"I was thinking of you when I named him and my mare. I had to leave Delilah with the show." A frown creased her brow, leaving him to believe she was concerned about what she'd left behind. Either that, or she was a mighty fine actress. "What's the name of the sweet-tempered mare tethered outside the corral?"

Hell if he'd admit his roan's name was Lila.

Calhoun raised an imperial-high eyebrow. "Your silence means you have recognized your error. You agree my wife is Jane Dority."

"Never will you convince me she's Jane." They could tell him lies all day, but Eldora's eyes held the truth. They weren't Jane's.

"Give me time," she said.

*Time?* He had none to give. He had ten horses to train in twenty-one days. A daunting task that required his full attention. He may want Eldora to stay, but she had to go.

He forced himself to speak. "Get off my land."

"You mean my wife's land. You'd deny her of her inheritance?"

His gut clenched with disbelief, then understanding. "You've been to Austin." Its land office held a copy of the deed along with the Doritys' signed and witnessed sale stipulation. If Jane returned and wanted the land instead of the trust fund they'd created with the sale income, the transaction was reversed.

Calhoun's smile turned smug. "You only own the land if Jane does not return."

"I'd gladly hand back the land to the real Jane if she stood before me." Anger heated his blood. "She's not here. So I want you both to leave."

"Bet I can change your mind." Eldora's words chilled him like raindrops from a distant storm.

"If you were Jane," he said very slowly, "you'd know I don't like to bet."

But Jane had. Her words joined the deluge needling him.

*Bet your father takes you next year. Bet you're as tall as Noah next year.*

The year after her disappearance, Jane had won her bets. And for eighteen years, he'd waited to tell her about the roundup, how he'd grown to love horses more than cattle, and how much he wanted to say he was sorry for driving her away.

"Sometimes you need to gamble to get what you want." Eldora's voice had turned soft and cajoling.

He fought her allure. "And what do I want?"

"First off"—she gestured toward the corral—"those horses trained in three weeks."

*Hellfire.* He was up against a master manipulator. "You've been mighty busy gathering information in Juniper Flats as well as in Austin."

"Bet you those Rangers will be *mighty pleased* to have horses that won't toss them in the dirt. I could help with that."

He felt his jaw drop.

"You will do no such thing," Calhoun roared. "Your place is with my show."

Eldora's gaze remained on him. "Bet you I can train more horses than you can. And if I can't, you can keep the land."

Lewis could only gape at her.

"He will not keep anything, because you will only do what I say. You will obey my command." Calhoun planted his hands on his hips. "You are my *wife*."

The word made Eldora flinch. Her hands shook as she grabbed her horse's reins and saddle horn, preparing to mount. With her back to him, she went suddenly still. "Is that why you won't bet with me? You're only interested in telling others what to do instead of listening?" Her voice grew strained. "Go on then. Tell me one last time. Tell me to get off your land. Tell me to *get out of your head.*"

The truth hit him hard. This woman was not Jane, but she was using Jane's words. Deliberately and also covertly. She was trying to tell him something. One final time. Before Calhoun forced her to leave.

She knew Jane. She knew her well. She might even know where Jane was right now. Eldora Calhoun represented his first chance of finding Jane.

He'd waited eighteen years for such a chance. No matter what happened, he couldn't let this woman leave.

"Mr. Adams will not bet with you because he is not a gambling man. So be silent! Can you not see his dislike for your wager equals mine?"

Calhoun was right. Leaving something so important to a game of chance went against his nature. Jane had wanted to bet with him all the time. Noah's wife was a gambler as well.

Sadie had gambled her way free of a life of sin in Dodge City. He could use her unique perspective and Noah's familiar straightforward advice right now. He needed help, but his friends' ranch was an hour's ride away. Eldora stood only a stride away, offering to work beside him. All he had to do was wager the land he loved.

"This meeting was a waste of time." Calhoun strode toward his horse. "One more night in that dreary town, then we ride on and rejoin the world. My lawyer will deal with you, Mr. Adams."

Before Eldora could put her toe in her stirrup, Lewis said, "I accept your wager. Whoever trains the most horses in three weeks wins the land."

She spun to face him, eyes shining with joy but also relief.

He held out his hand.

Without hesitation, she reached to take it.

"No!" Calhoun barked, halting her midway. "I will not allow it."

Lewis kept his hand extended. "I won't tell you what to do, but I have one condition: you have to be here—standing on Dority land—twenty-one days from now in order to win."

As handshakes went, hers was the best he had ever received. It filled him with warmth and happiness. Feeling like a besotted fool, he released her abruptly and folded his arms across his chest to keep from taking hold of her again.

A frown pinched her brow. Was she regretting her wager already, or was she offended by the way he'd dropped her hand like a flaming hot coal?

"Maybe we can both win."

What did she mean? There could only be one winner; one owner of the land.

"No bet. No deal. Mount up," Calhoun ordered. "We are leaving."

"If she leaves, you lose. That's the deal."

"A deal that can be undone." Calhoun slashed the air with his hand.

"Roy, give me a chance to learn why this land is so important."

Surprise held Lewis mute. If they didn't believe the land had value, why were they here? Why not arrange to receive the trust fund while they'd been in Austin and hurry back to their show? What had made Eldora suggest her wager and agree to stay with him for three weeks?

"You will discover nothing of significance up here." Calhoun's voice was firm and certain. "All you need remember is that this land is a birthright and a future. We are within our rights to reclaim it. Better now than later."

"Awful impatient, aren't you?" Lewis asked. "What's the hurry? You took your sweet time getting here, only arriving after Jane's parents passed."

"We are here now. We are disputing your ownership. The land belongs to my wife."

"Land you won't even live on for a few weeks."

"I am needed elsewhere."

"Then go. My wager is with her, not you."

"She cannot stay here." Calhoun waved his hand in the air. "There isn't even a house to live in."

"There's a cabin." Eldora stared at the structure with a mixture of curiosity and doubt.

Calhoun jabbed his finger at Lewis. "And where will he stay?"

"At my family's ranch." He'd lose two hours riding there and back each day. Those hours lost would help Eldora win. But if she helped him make the horses ready for the Rangers, he wouldn't let those men down. If he failed them, word of mouth would travel. No one would ever buy anything from him again. And rightfully so.

If he really wanted to save time and keep a proper watch on Eldora, he should spread his bedroll outside the cabin by the fire pit. The thought made him smile.

Calhoun's glare grew ominous. He snatched the reins from Eldora's hand. Her previously docile giant of a horse reared and yanked the big man off his feet.

"Roy, release Samson! You know he doesn't like—"

"Allow me, Colonel." Vandrill grabbed the reins.

Calhoun let go as soon as he did, and Samson calmed just as quickly. Eldora did not. Her hand trembled again. This time, as she stroked her horse's neck.

Calhoun's expression turned calculating. "How do we proceed from here, Mr. Vandrill?"

The pointed look that passed between the two men raised the hair on Lewis' neck.

Vandrill inclined his head toward the corral. "Shall I tether Samson out of the way so that I, as your lawyer, may advise you unimpeded?"

Calhoun gave a curt nod. "Eldora, go inside that hovel" —he flicked his fingers toward the cabin—"you wish to call home for nearly a month. Ponder its dearth of comforts and amusements on which we both thrive. Do not come out until summoned. Leave me and Mr. Vandrill alone to discuss your wager."

# CHAPTER 2

The Dority cabin, disheveled and wild as its new owner and the surrounding hillside, reminded Eldora of the mountain men who joined the show but never stayed long.

A jumble of tack, tools, and tinned food covered the floor and lined the surprisingly tall walls. The space sucked her in, enveloped her...and soothed her nerves like the embrace of the caravan she'd called home till she turned eighteen. The second time her life had changed. The year she'd married Roy.

Last week her world had spun again, like a child's pinwheel facing a foul wind. She'd finally held the coveted papers that ended her ten-year marriage only to be shown a letter that bound her as firmly as ever to Roy. She couldn't refute the title of Mrs. Calhoun. Not if she wanted to protect what mattered most. And that wasn't her well-being or the show's.

Once she'd prayed only for talent, the chance to perform, the fleeting moments to earn an audience's approval. She'd worked hard for their every cheer until she bound her happiness to the limelight of Roy's show...now camped out of reach, three towns and two rivers away.

If those waterways had risen higher than slumbering creeks not yet awakened by the spring runoff, her fear of water may have kept her from reaching the Dority homestead. The recent memory of those crossings and the long ago nightmare of the Mississippi settled like a boulder on her chest.

The wall of rock surrounding the corrals like a horseshoe with its opening near the cabin deepened her anxiety, threatening to suffocate her. The endless press of trees on either side of the narrow trail leading down to Juniper Flats didn't help. Nature might be beautiful, but it could also be cruel.

She didn't want this land. Neither did Roy. But they had agreed to come here to save what they each cherished most. So why was Roy now so opposed to staying? Why the sudden need to make her leave this land and Juniper Flats as well? What did he hope to hide, and why couldn't he tell her everything?

Concern for her loved ones, Samson included, rang in her head like a warning bell. Why had Roy taken him from her and told her to go inside this cabin?

She made a beeline for the doorway but forced herself to stop there, to lean against the doorjamb and wait. Across a wide expanse of dirt, but only a dozen strides from the corrals, Roy and Vandrill conversed.

What was Roy up to now?

Samson hovered beside Lewis' horse. Out of reach of Roy. She sighed with relief, then smiled. Even though Lewis Adams wouldn't admit it, she suspected his mare's name was Delilah.

All these years, he'd remembered: Scout and Sergeant,

the childhood wonder of being told the tale of Samson. And Delilah. He'd held tight to his memories of Jane.

For an all-too-brief moment, Eldora had basked in the steadfast rancher's affection, hoping it might shine on her for real and not be a reflection of his feelings for Jane. The way he hadn't blinked as his hazel-green gaze held hers, the way he'd described her plain brown eyes, the way he'd hung on her every word...until Roy intruded and made Lewis interested in her in a completely different way.

He wanted his old friend back. The Jane he'd known was gone.

The young boy longing to grow tall that Lewis had been was gone as well. She'd do well to remember that everyone changed and most, even those carving a living beyond show caravans and tents, put on acts.

The spring sun glinted in the treetops and the tall Texan's golden hair as he returned to his work. He untied his strawberry roan, led her through the gate and into the corral.

On the other side, Samson pushed against the planks, irked to be left behind. Lewis paused to run a slow hand over Samson's neck and his long, braided mane. Whenever they traveled, Eldora spent hours keeping the lengthy strands tidy and tangle free.

Lewis had invested a similar amount of time on his mare. She glowed like polished pale rose granite, like she'd recently received a thorough grooming. Unlike her master, whose wind-swept hair resembled a wheat field in want of a farmer's scythe. In fact, all of Lewis looked in need of a helping hand.

How long had he been up here working alone?

When Samson settled, Lewis led his mare over to the wild-eyed Appaloosa who'd thrown him. He now stroked his mare's neck. His lips moved as well. The memory of his seductive drawl when she'd first found him lying on the ground soothed her like a soft summer day.

The Appaloosa grew increasingly still and silent, but his eyes remained on the man. He didn't trust him, but he took comfort from the other horse's acceptance of his direct but also easy manner...as Eldora had done.

Lewis Adams couldn't approach anyone in an under-handed way. He had compassion as well as courage. Her rebuke about trying to ride the Appaloosa before earning the horse's trust made her cringe. She'd judged Lewis unfairly, and he'd accepted her wager even though it wasn't in his best interest.

She had three weeks to learn why this land was so important. She'd come because Jane couldn't. Without her meddling, Jane might have come home ten years ago. Now Jane wouldn't, so Eldora had to pretend to be Jane. She must stay here for Jane and for all the people she'd hurt with her selfishness, including Lewis and the Doritys. Jane's parents may have passed, but Eldora still hoped to do right by them.

A loud pop followed by an ear-piercing whinny and crash yanked her attention back to Samson.

Vandrill, Roy's prized marksman, was as accurate with a pebble as with a bullet. She didn't need to see his slingshot to know it had made Samson smash through the corral and send Lewis' horses racing like a river through the hole—toward the trail leading into the trees. Once there, the herd would be impossible to stop and would take weeks to round up.

Roy had found a way to undo her wager. Without those horses, she had no reason to stay on Dority land. She'd have to return to town and then the show. She might find her answers there.

But Lewis would remain here, on the homestead he cherished. Not for long. He'd lose the money from the sale to the Rangers, and Roy would continue using her to ensure Lewis lost his land.

He'd suffer once again for what she'd done, and not done.

She whistled for Samson, yanked her skirt from the hooks custom-made for the sole purpose of swiftly casting aside the restraining fabric. The trousers underneath made it easier to sprint into the path of the stampeding horses.

LED by the blasted Appaloosa Cayuse, Lewis' horses spilled through the hole Samson had busted in the corral. The volatile stallion crowded him and Lila into a corner, shielding and hemming them in at the same time. Whatever had spooked the horse, he'd gone from needing protection to offering it in a heartbeat.

Either way, he was ensuring Lewis lost everything.

A shrill whistle whipped Samson around and sent him thundering after the last horse departing the corral. Lewis leapt onto Lila bareback and gave chase.

Samson plowed a path straight through the river of heaving horse flesh. Lewis slipped Lila into his wake. The brute had become Lewis' best chance to avert disaster. If he could catch the lead horse, the Appaloosa, and turn him, his followers might embrace their herd mentality and turn as well.

Lewis scanned the distance remaining between the stampede and the trail.

Eldora Calhoun stood dead ahead. Disbelief then fear sent Lewis' heart racing as fast as the herd. Horses usually tried to avoid running over people or anything that made for unstable footing—if they weren't spooked witless.

Eldora couldn't stop them. She was going to get herself killed. Unless Lewis reached her before the horses did.

Samson pulled ahead to run even with the Appaloosa. Lewis urged Lila to move up beside the pair, but the herd jostled Lila sideways, away from Samson, hemming them in again, leaving him unable to reach Eldora.

Finally, she moved.

Pivoting sideways, she braced one foot behind her and raised her hands as if preparing to grasp something in front of her...where nothing existed but air. Never once had her gaze left Samson.

Understanding made his heart leap with hope. She intended to mount Samson on the run.

A second later, Samson's bulk blocked his view. Then her hand flashed on the horn and she bounded up onto the saddle.

She'd made it look easy. It wasn't. Especially considering Samson's speed, his height, and the threat thundering behind him. The herd surged forward. Soon they'd sweep by Samson like a river 'round a rock. Once they reached the trees, they'd scatter and take a heap of time to catch.

Strangely, it didn't seem so important anymore. Not with Eldora out of danger.

She freed a coil of rope tied to her saddle, shook out a lariat and swung it over her head, once, twice, building speed. She dropped her noose over the Appaloosa's head, looped the other end around her horn and let the line yank tight.

A grin lifted his lips. She planned to turn the lead horse and the herd. Angel Eyes was one helluva horsewoman.

As if he'd called her name, she glanced over her

shoulder and returned his smile. Then she inclined her head to the right. As soon as he nodded, she turned Samson and the Appaloosa. He followed with Lila, using her body as a barricade and incentive to encourage any would-be rebels to join the flow.

Behind him, the herd turned in a smooth arc. Except for a gangly colt that darted free. His mother followed. That was all it took for the foal to continue toward the trail, and for the duo to disappear into the trees.

Getting the rest of the herd back into the corral took patience and teamwork. He urged Lila in front of any potential escapees, but he couldn't reach them all. Every time he didn't, Eldora was there, and when she halted Samson in the break in the fence, he knew she was there to stay.

He ran to retrieve a hammer and a pail of nails. When he returned, he couldn't help but chuckle. The entire herd, including their Appaloosa ringleader, hugged the back of the corral while casting curious looks at Samson but also staying clear of him.

Lewis' good humor fled when he spotted Calhoun and his guard Vandrill standing well out the way—up near the rocks where they'd retreated to watch the show. This was no show. This was real. Eldora could have been killed.

Standing beside her, still mounted on Samson, Lewis bent to inspect the busted planks. He kept his head down, not wanting her to see the anger and fear and disbelief churning inside him. "What if you hadn't made that mount?"

"The odds were in my favor." Her voice was soft and soothing.

He knew that tone. He used it to calm his horses.

He attacked the splintered end of the first plank with his hammer. "You like to gamble too much." You could've died.

Her whisper of a sigh barely reached his ears. "Nothing ventured, nothing gained."

"You bet your life." To help me. He yanked the remains of the other two planks free of the post.

"I bet on Samson. We've practiced that mount many times."

Samson snorted and sidestepped into him. Lewis moved around to his other side to see what had unsettled the horse this time. Calhoun and Vandrill scrambled down from their vantage point, heading toward the corral.

"Hey," Lewis called, "since you're already up there, how about lending a hand and retrieving three planks from the pile behind you?"

Their extended staring match only ended when Calhoun and Vandrill turned back to do as asked.

Lewis went to work on the other side of the hole, preparing for the new planks and trying to understand the whirlwind that was Eldora Calhoun or—what had she called herself?—Eldorado Jane, a trick rider in a show that had entertained all of New York.

"You're telling me that you and Samson practice with a stampede bearing down on you?"

"Yes. And before you ask, yes—most of the horses have riders, and the buffalo occasionally does as well. But the elk, of course, never had."

Heaven help him. The lady came from the land of the loco. How had she survived unscathed this long? He tried to cover his concern with a quip. "Had? What happened to the elk? Did he dislike the stampede and run away?"

"He enjoyed running with the herd very much. We could never stop him from joining. We lost him ten years ago on the Mississippi, heading to New Orleans to merge our show with Roy's."

The word "lost" sent a chill of apprehension up his spine. He straightened his back and let his hammer dangle by his side. Calhoun and his guard had covered half the distance to the corral. The scrape of the wood they dragged disturbed his already unsettled nerves.

"Your elk didn't want to team up with Calhoun, so he swam off?" he asked hopefully.

"He drowned when our steamboat struck another and sank. We lost many friends that day."

"I'm sorry. I wish—" He stopped short of saying he wished he'd been there to help save every one of her friends. If an elk was important to her, it was important to him.

Lord help him, he was a damned fool. She'd come to take his land, and he wanted to be her knight in shining armor.

He finally turned to face her. He couldn't stare at the damage to his corral any longer while trying to avoid getting lost in looking at her. He tried to keep his gaze off the shape of her legs revealed by her trousers. He focused on her face. "Don't do anything like that again, no matter how good the odds are."

Her lips twitched, then flattened as her chin rose to a rebellious angle. "I thought you said you wouldn't tell me what to do?"

"When it comes to keeping you and Samson safe, ignore all my promises."

Soft laughter cascaded from her lips. The sound made everything right in the world until the growing grate of dragging wood drowned out the sweet sound.

He needed to get Eldora alone so they could talk uninterrupted and without the chance of Calhoun overhearing. He needed to ask her why she'd truly come here. He wanted to learn everything she knew about Jane. But he also needed to go after his runaways.

"Will you be able to retrieve your mare and foal?"

Once again, she'd read his mind. Either that, or she'd caught his glance at the forest.

"Depends how fast I can leave. Need to fix this fence first."

Calhoun and Vandrill dropped their planks by the corral. Calhoun had brought one, while his guard had brought two. Vandrill might be lean, but he was strong.

Lewis grabbed the end of one plank and held the man's ice-blue gaze. "Care to hold one end in place while I hammer in the other?"

Vandrill complied without a glance at his boss. Lewis grudgingly gave him credit for that. Eldora backed Samson up, but only enough to give them room to work. After Vandrill helped replace the remaining two planks, Lewis thanked him and crossed the few strides to where Eldora remained mounted on Samson.

"Thank you for helping retrieve my herd." He patted Samson's neck. "And you, you big lug, thank you for keeping your mistress safe, but no more breaking down my corral."

"That animal," Calhoun muttered, "needs a firmer hand than my wife possesses."

"I will never allow anyone to take a firm hand to Samson." Eldora's voice had turned hard as iron. "I told you that when I removed him from Buckley's Circus of horrors." Her gaze cut to Roy's guard. "I don't know why Samson trusts you, Mr. Vandrill. I don't."

Vandrill didn't move a muscle, but something flickered in his eyes. Or maybe it was simply a trick of the sun...which was heading toward the horizon too fast.

Calhoun didn't bother to hide his glare. "Didn't I tell you to stay in the cabin?"

"Ah, yes, what did you think of your new home?" Lewis didn't pause to let her answer. He didn't want to hear her dislike for the tiny cabin he loved. "Jane's father built it to last. It's as sturdy as it is cozy and...rustic. That's probably the word your husband would use. I imagine it could use a few luxuries from town." He checked the sun's height again. "There's barely enough daylight to ride to Juniper Flats and back. Waste any more time and you'll be roughing it all night in that cabin."

"Retrieve our horses, Mr. Vandrill."

When his guard did as bid, Calhoun mounted the showy white and Vandrill the more practical bay.

Good. The moment they left, he could go after his runaways. Regret pierced him at the prospect of Eldora leaving as well, even for a few hours. His regret spiked into worry. What if she didn't return?

"If Eldora wishes to honor her wager, she'd best come back."

"I will return with my wife and my lawyer."

Lewis shrugged as if he didn't really care. Only one thought gave authenticity to his attempt at nonchalance: if she didn't return, the first thing he'd do was ride straight to town and find her. "Well, now that the show's over and"—he locked his gaze on Calhoun—"you stayed on the sidelines and missed your perfect opportunity to ride circles around me, I'll say goodbye."

The three riders headed for the trail. Lewis strode toward Lila, wishing with every step that Eldora would be riding by his side for the next hours instead of her husband's.

Her honeyed voice drifted back to him. "Good thing

there'll be three of us to clean that cabin when we return. A pigeon coop couldn't be more dirty or smelly."

Disbelief snapped his spine straight. His cabin wasn't that bad. He may be a rustic and not the tidiest of people, but he kept things clean. Or at least he thought he did. How had he left the cabin this morning? He hadn't expected visitors.

Gritting his teeth against a useless defense, he saddled Lila.

Unfortunately, the view over Lila's back was of Calhoun. The colonel remained the center of his world, with his wife riding on one side and his lawyer on the other. None of them looked back.

Eldora had already forgotten about him, but not her new home. "That cabin," she continued, "will probably take as long to clean as it does to ride to town and back."

Calhoun jerked his mount to a halt. The other horses stopped as well. "Then you had best stay behind and complete the task before Mr. Vandrill and I return. Honor our agreement while I'm gone. If you do not play your part..." He glanced over his shoulder at Lewis. "I will know." Calhoun kicked his mount into a full gallop and charged down the trail.

His guard followed. The two men disappeared into the trees, leaving Lewis alone with Eldora.

Finally, he was going to get his answers. He'd find out where Jane was.

Eldora turned in her saddle and leaned on the palm she planted on Samson's black rump. Her smile was so bright it blinded him and trapped his breath in his lungs again.

"Since your cabin's only shortcomings are space and clutter, I wonder if my time could be better spent elsewhere."

Eldora Calhoun had lied about being Jane, but Angel Eyes had lied to stay with him...at least for the next few hours. No, they had weeks. And like his horses, he'd find a way to work with her, to earn her trust, and get to the truth —which was buried under many mysterious layers. He must proceed slowly. He mustn't reveal his eagerness. He didn't want to spook her.

He tried to stifle his smile. And failed.

"Daylight's burning," she called out in her sweet voice.

Yes, it was—along with every fiber of his body. He felt more rattled than she sounded.

"How about I help retrieve your horses?" she asked. "Shall we set aside our differences and play partners for a few hours?"

*artners.* Using the word to entice Lewis into agreeing they ride together kindled a spark inside Eldora. His grin fanned the flame, and then he laughed. A deep sound richer than any compliment or even the combined cheer of a thousand-strong crowd. Lewis' happiness resonated in her blood. He made her heart race.

For the first time in a decade, her cheeks grew warm.

Heaven help her, she hadn't blushed even when Buffalo Bill Cody praised her talent with horses. Thinking about the famous scout and occasional showman always propelled her thoughts to the future. Nothing could help her and Roy if Cody decided to form his own show. He'd steal their audience.

Luckily, Cody was currently occupied scouting for the army, taking bigwigs on staged hunts, and presenting plays with his sometimes partners, Texas Jack and Ned Buntline. A partner could be a blessing or a curse. Which type was Lewis? Which was she?

He led his roan over to stand beside Samson and stared at her for a long moment before he said, "Before we go anywhere, shouldn't we talk? Jane once told me that the best partners act in harmony."

Jane had told her that as well. *Bless the day you came into my life, Jane Dority. Curse it as well for putting you beside me on a sinking steamboat. You should've stayed on solid land. With Lewis by your side.*

He would've kept Jane safe. His untamed hair and simple clothing couldn't hide his wealth of character. She shouldn't have been surprised he'd acted so swiftly during the stampede and remained so concerned afterward.

His ready smile was another matter. He probably had plenty of practice with all sorts of stampedes, especially women chasing after him. Just like Roy.

Her continued silence brought an inquiring arc to Lewis' eyebrows. "You said we needed to talk before your companions joined us. Well, they're gone now. So, what did you want to tell me?"

*I've come to protect Jane. To succeed, I must hurt you, deceive you, steal from you.* The stories Jane had told and retold her over the years had made her hope Lewis would join her side of the battle. She'd raced ahead of Roy to find out. Instead, she'd discovered Lewis' reactions—and his one attempt at deception involving Sergeant's name—revealed plain as day on his honest face. This was a man with little skill for lying.

Roy saw it, too. *Honor our agreement while I'm gone*, he'd said. *If you do not, I will know.*

She must embrace her lies again, including the one she'd recently told Roy. When he'd demanded to know if she was Jane Dority, she'd said, yes.

If she didn't maintain all of her lies, Roy would share no more letters with her. She'd never learn why this land had suddenly become so important to the anonymous man blackmailing Roy to steal it for him.

They followed the blackmailer's demands for different reasons. Roy would guard his show and the goldmine that was the Eldorado Jane act. She'd shield Jane from any future turmoil. The blackmailer wouldn't look Jane's way if he believed Eldora was Jane, and that she and Roy were working diligently to get the land for him.

"Shouldn't we talk *later?*" she asked, knowing later often became never. "You said finding your mare and foal depended on going after them quickly." Her manipulations may have slipped from her lips with ease, but they were starting to weigh like a stone on her heart.

Especially when Lewis stared at her like he understood every detail of her ruse. Her muscles clenched unbearably tight as she waited for him to call her a liar.

"Well, partner," he drawled, "tell me to slow down if Samson can't keep up with..." He shook his head and gave her a lopsided smile. "Lila."

Delight and relief that he'd changed the topic eased her worries. "Samson," she said with a firm nod, "will always be able to keep up with Lila, and Delilah."

"Eldora..." His smile grew strained. "Up here, you need to be careful. This isn't New York, and where I'm heading, the land only gets rougher."

She pressed her palm to her heart. "I promise I won't slow you down."

"That's not what concerns me." He spun on his heel and went into the cabin. When he came out, he had a handgun strapped to his hip and an old Henry rifle, which he secured in a scabbard on his saddle. He paused to hold her gaze. "Ready?"

When she nodded, he leapt onto Lila and headed for the trail.

Her confidence fled when he led her uphill and the

wilderness swallowed them. Only watching Lewis navigate swiftly through the trees and underbrush as he searched for and found tracks steadied her.

On an outcrop, they paused to let the horses catch their breath. Below them, a craggy panorama of red rock overrun with thickets gradually gave way to meadows blanketed in bluebonnets. A whitewater river rumbled out of a deep ravine, turning glossier and flatter the closer it came to the distant speck of Juniper Flats.

She searched for the Dority homestead, but couldn't see it. "We'll never get back to the cabin before nightfall."

"I'll get you home safely. You have my word." His lips twitched. "I cannot, however, guarantee you'll have time to clean the cabin before your husband returns."

She fought the desire to tell him that Roy was no longer her husband. That truth wouldn't help her win the land and Jane's well-being.

Although some shows thrived on scandal, Roy's had been built on his image as an honorable war hero. His unwillingness to have his many infidelities paraded out in the papers had been the key to making him agree to a divorce, as long as she kept silent and signed an indefinite contract with the show. She might no longer want to live as man and wife with Roy, but he knew she needed the show's limelight.

Now she needed something even more. She needed to pretend to be married to Roy in order to keep the blackmailer's focus on her and Roy, and not Jane.

When she failed to respond to Lewis' teasing about her comments concerning his cabin, a frown marred his brow. "Why didn't you go with Calhoun? Why did you lie to stay with me?"

"I need to learn more about this land and you."

"Finally!" The word burst from his lips with relief and laughter. "You admit you don't know me."

Her carelessness made her stiffen. She'd be wise to put a barrier between. "I know the boy you were, Mr. Adams, not the man you've become."

He considered her carefully before he spoke, or maybe he was trying to be careful with his words. "You'll learn all you need to know if you stay and train those horses with me, because I'll be by your side every day doing the same." His smile returned, and his tone turned teasing. "And you'll get more information out of me if you call me Lewis. I'll think you're talking to someone else if you call me Mr. Adams. That's what Jane called my father."

An intense desire to learn everything about this man blossomed in her heart. What had happened after he'd lost Jane in the storm?

"Your father and mother, and your sisters..." She searched for their names. "Olivia and Oralee. I hope they are all well."

"We've had our share of challenges, but that's the way life is out here—challenging whether I ride on my family's land, the Dority's, or a field outside Juniper Flats." He turned Lila to tackle the ascent again. "Let's see where our current challenges are. That mare and foal can't climb much farther before reaching the headwaters."

Unease slithered down her spine as their horses slogged up the slope. The wind gusted against her face, smothering her with the scent of damp earth and rock, and the rumble of water tumbling, falling...as if into a deep chasm.

With an uncharacteristically hard hand on the reins, Lewis halted his mare. Samson stopped as well. "Go back, Eldora."

"Why?" She craned her neck to see around them.

"Last week this path was a creek. Dead ahead there's only a sinkhole."

So much for standing on solid ground. She'd been short-sighted to believe nothing could rival her fear of the Mississippi.

"Turn Samson around. Now." The urgency in his voice made her comply.

She froze halfway when she glimpsed the dark crevasse ahead and, hovering beside it, the mare and foal. Quivering with fright. Ready to leap. Not away from the hole, but across it. An impossible stretch for the young colt.

Lewis slid his rifle from the scabbard. "Go to the cabin or to town. Either will do. Just go and don't look back."

She couldn't go. She couldn't stop staring at him. Until his gaze shifted, and hers followed his along with the tip of his rifle. They looked away from the mare and foal, tracking the direction the mare kept glancing, to the ridge above Lewis.

The tawny head and spine of a mountain lion rose from the rock, preparing to descend on Lewis. Fangs bared, the big cat paused, shifting its weight, favoring one leg.

The click of Lewis' rifle being cocked sent the cat flat against the ridge again. Only its hiss fell on them. It knew the sting of the metal rod Lewis pointed at it. Was that what had injured its leg?

She yanked her derringer from its hiding place under the ruffle at the back of her jacket and pointed it at the top of the ridge. Steadying the gun with both hands, she extended her arms as far as she could.

For the first time, she wished she'd invested as much time in firearms as in horses. She'd bought the palm pistol to discourage overzealous or inebriated show guests. The miniature gun was only accurate if its target came close.

Using her knees, she nudged Samson nearer to Lila and Lewis. If he missed his shot, she would not.

"Eldora." Her name sprang from his lips like the snarl of a cornered animal. When he fell silent, so did the air above them.

"Is it gone?" Her whispered words hung between them.

Lewis glanced at the mare. She scuttled away from the hole and herded her foal toward them.

"For now." He lowered his rifle. "Why didn't you leave as I asked?" His glare dissolved into astonished disbelief when he turned in his saddle to stare at her. "What the blazes did you intend to accomplish with that toy?"

"I'm fully aware of my derringer's limitations, especially in a situation such as this. But the instant that cat landed on you, it would've felt this barrel"—she shook the tiny weapon at him like a disapproving finger—"hard against its neck and then it would have felt nothing more."

"Hellfire and tarnation, woman! You could turn a man's hair white with your daredevil ways."

She blinked back the sudden sting of tears and stared at the mare and foal trotting by Samson and down the slope. "Being angry with me won't change anything."

"I'm not angry with you, but with what you do." His voice, equal parts soothing and gruff, caressed her ear, as did his deep sigh of resignation.

"I cannot change who I am. Or who I'm not." She reined Samson aside so Lewis could pass by and follow the mare and foal.

"Eldora." The deeply sad way he said her name made her shoulders sag. "Tell me about Jane."

She drew herself up. "Don't make me say any more. It's not your fault, but you're a terrible liar. If you knew everything, Roy would stop confiding in me. I must act like his partner if I wish to discover the importance of your land."

"Your life and Jane's are more important than any land."

Finally, she turned to look at him. The smile curving his lips made her jaw drop. "You'd gamble your land for *me*?"

His smile remained. "I already did, and I'd gamble a lot more. This time, I'm keeping both you and Jane safe." Still holding his rifle at the ready, he unbuckled his revolver belt and handed it to her. "Wear this at all times. Your palm pistol might be adequate for New York, but in Texas we require something larger."

As soon as she'd accepted his offering, he gestured with his rifle for her to precede him down the hill. "Until we reach the cabin, you stay in front of me. I'll tell you if you wander off the trail." He scanned the ridge behind them and those ahead as well.

She urged Samson to catch up with the mare and foal. Lila's hooves sounded close behind.

"Will the cat stay in the highland?" she asked.

"Until hunger makes him desperate. Then he'll come down."

"To the Dority homestead?"

"Or my family's place, or Noah and Sadie's." His tone turned somber. "As soon as you're secure in the cabin, I'll have to go warn them."

She didn't want him to go anywhere. Only the sound of him and Lila close behind her, for now, kept her voice steady. "Does Noah still live on his ranch next to your family's?"

"He does. That creek bed, the one that is now a big sinkhole, used to run to his land."

"And Sadie is his wife?"

"Yes."

"I'm glad to hear he's not alone. I always hoped he'd find happiness after losing his parents so young." An inexorable impulse made her ask, "How come he's married and you aren't?"

Before she could tell him to ignore her nosiness, he replied. "Noah met Sadie in Dodge a couple of years ago. Ever since, they've only had eyes for each other. I hadn't understood that feeling until—" His low growl swallowed whatever he'd meant to say.

"Until?"

"No use dwelling on what we cannot have. Let's talk about something else. Better yet, let's *do* something." He let out a whoop like one of the Sioux riders in Roy's show. "Let's race! Dazzle me with your brilliance, Eldorado Jane. Show me how fast you can get home to our cabin."

ELDORA REARRANGED THE CABIN, stacking items by content, shape, and size while Roy paced the slivers of space she'd cleared, muttering a litany of complaints and grievances. Her thoughts were just as restless, circling back to one. Lewis calling the cabin not his or hers, but ours.

Last night, he'd said something heartbreakingly similar. After Roy and Vandrill had returned. Before he'd ridden Lila into the dark. "This is a good cabin. It'll protect you while I'm gone." He'd glanced at Roy and lowered his voice so only she could hear. "There's another rifle and revolver under the bed, plus enough bullets to stop a hundred mountain lions or heartless husbands and their men. You'll be safe until—" Hesitation narrowed his eyes.

"Until?"

He'd shaken his head and finally smiled. When he'd

walked away, his words had come over his shoulder like a vow. "You're safe till I get home and our wager starts in earnest."

A loud thump followed by a yelp interrupted her musings.

Roy clutched his knee. In crowded spaces, he wasn't agile on his feet, but he was a masterful rider, a decent shot and had started practicing knife throwing, which showed that even a prominent impresario in charge of producing acts might one day wish to participate in them again. Not that she wanted Roy to take over Tomahawk Joe's duties. The Lakota knifeman, who preferred to be called Hawk outside of the show ring, had joined them last year and was better with blades that anyone Eldora had seen.

Roy spewed a lengthy and colorful stream of curses until he had to pause for breath. "I detest this place. Even the lowliest of army barracks would be better."

"Why don't you step outside and get some air?"

Roy jabbed his finger at the world beyond the cabin door. "I won't go out there until Vandrill returns."

She'd never seen him so jittery, so...scared. What was out there that he feared? It wasn't a mountain lion or Mother Nature. What couldn't he face until Vandrill returned?

At first light, Roy had sent his guard back to town. Vandrill had gone eagerly after having to sleep in a bedroll on the cabin floor the night before.

The cramped interior didn't bother her, but sleeping next to Roy on the narrow bed had. His current frenetic energy was equally unsettling. If she was going to endure any more time in this cabin with him, she needed to create space to move and breathe.

She started on the sacks, making separate piles for

human and horse, trying to act like receiving an answer to her next question wasn't important. "What happened in town yesterday?"

"Nothing you need know about."

"Don't shut me out, Roy. We made a good team once. Together we can beat this blackmailer."

"You have chosen your path. A solitary one. You shall walk it alone until instructed otherwise, Little Miss Hoity-Toity."

The name hit her like a bucket of water. Left her trembling and clasping a sack of flour against her chest like a shield.

Only once before had he called her that...ten years ago, when they'd first met. When the nightmare of the Mississippi shrouded her every move, made her feel more dead than alive. Then Gaylon explained the accident, and Roy had become the most caring and devoted of guardians. She'd fallen for the finest act a showman had ever presented.

"Play your part," he added. "Only then may we return to our routine. I'm not without compassion. I won't replace you."

"You already did, many times, with your women."

"None of them ever took what you loved most—your limelight in the show. But you took your friend Dory's."

A rising foreboding made her clutch the sack even tighter. Not long after they'd first met, Jane had insisted that everyone call her Dory. Eldora had impulsively decided she should be called Doro. That was their first step toward becoming as close as twins. Their real names had been forgotten, and the name Jane hadn't been uttered until they'd created the Eldorado Jane act.

Roy always knew Eldora wasn't the original performer of

the act, but she rode well enough that he'd never cared or spoken a word about how she'd so easily taken over the act.

Until now.

Roy's smile grew into a smirk. "Deep down, you've always been heartless."

His words robbed her of breath. The honorable man she'd pledged her love and her life to was long gone. Maybe he'd never existed. Only the spiteful philanderer remained.

The clatter of fast approaching hooves echoed outside. She dropped the sack and surged toward the door, like a drowning swimmer in search of air.

"Halt!" Roy's shout rattled the cabin behind her. "You've no idea what's out there."

She had one idea, one wish. *Lewis. Please let it be Lewis coming home.* Her spark of hope crumbled into ash when a pair of familiar riders and mounts appeared. Vandrill on his bay. Hawk on his black and white pinto.

A new fear swamped her. Why wasn't Hawk with the show?

She sprinted toward him. "Where's Dory? Is she—?"

"She's fine." With a hard yank on her arm, Roy halted her. Then, arms akimbo, he planted himself between her and the Lakota brave. "And you'll both stay fine if everyone heeds my orders. Return to the cabin. I will speak to my men uninterrupted."

She couldn't obey, couldn't move. She hadn't known Hawk long, but she'd always felt she could trust him. He'd never given her reason not to. She searched his face. The hard planes, smooth as the blade for which he was named, revealed nothing. Neither did his eyes, dark as his long hair, unfathomable as a river bottom.

Panic leapt in her throat and parted her lips on a silent cry.

Hawk's brows rose like startled raven wings. But it was his hands that took flight, forming two signals, swift and beautiful. Signs from his people, shared with her for when words failed in a show racing beyond control.

All. Safe.

The message settled her nerves and loosened her feet. She trudged back to her assigned position. She didn't resume her rearranging of the cabin, though. She stood on the threshold. On guard. For more signs.

Vandrill and Hawk dismounted and talked calmly. Roy did not. With a slash of his hand, he ordered Hawk toward the smallest corral beside the cabin, where Samson and Roy's horse rested. Leading his pinto, Hawk ran ahead while Roy and Vandrill followed at a slower but still determined pace, talking until they reached the corral and came within range of her hearing them.

Hawk saddled Roy's white charger and handed the reins to him. When he turned to gather Samson, Roy halted him.

Hawk cast a puzzled glance her way. Vandrill's face remained unreadable.

"Eldora stays?" Hawk asked.

Roy nodded. "Her choice. Against my advice, she made a wager. She'd better be well on her way to winning when we return—which will be before nightfall."

The trio mounted in a flurry and galloped down the trail. Only Hawk raised his hand in farewell.

What had brought him here? What awaited them in town?

She wouldn't find out if she didn't follow. She could trail them at a distance, staying close enough to be out of sight but not alone.

Alone. Was that the real reason she felt compelled to

leave? Could she not be alone for even one day? Roy had said they'd return before nightfall.

The clatter of hooves grew silent. The stillness grew deafening. She raced to the corral, then clutched the fence post to stop from going farther.

*I will not be a puppet to loneliness. I will not be driven by fear.*

Her surroundings may have been new, but this battle was not. Only hard work, endless hours of training, had muted her anxiety, her need for love and acceptance.

She needed to lose herself in work. The notion seemed even lonelier than it had before.

Her gaze, searching for company, settled on the big corral and its inhabitants. She had plenty of horses to get to know. She chose a lively sorrel and, using her lasso, brought him into one of the medium-sized corrals. Then she freed him and took up her position on the opposite side of the enclosure.

"Bet by day's end you and I are the best of friends."

# CHAPTER 4

The height of the sun, approaching midday, fueled Lewis' worry as Lila labored up the hill toward the Dority homestead. To ease her load and make use of his nervous energy, he jumped down and tackled the ascent by her side.

Traveling at first light from his family's ranch to Noah and Sadie's to spread the warning about the mountain lion had been essential. But the visit that followed had consumed more time than the ride and the delivery of that one message. A visit he would have embraced wholeheartedly if his thoughts hadn't been in two places.

Sadie and Noah had been eager to show him everything their son had accomplished since his last visit. Jacob deserved his godfather's undivided attention, but Lewis had struggled to give it. Only watching the Ballantynes dote on their son had provided a fleeting but oh-so welcome respite from his obsession with Eldora.

He hadn't had the heart to interrupt their merriment with his troubles.

Until Sadie did, asking what occupied his mind. Telling

her the story of his childhood friend and how she vanished on that rainy night had taken more time.

Sadie and Noah's advice had not. They'd both agreed he should leave immediately and keep a close watch on the woman.

As he'd left, Sadie had followed him out of the house with a dozen of her fresh-baked biscuits and the whispered request that he check the headwaters feeding their ranch. The creek beds were dry, and even though Noah assured her spring's runoff was merely delayed, she knew he was worried. And so was she.

They should be. If too many branches of a ranch's water supply disappeared, the outcome would be grim. He shied away from telling her about the sinkhole that had devoured one of their creeks. It might mean nothing. He hoped it meant nothing.

But no water meant shriveled crops, dead livestock, and little hope of feeding your family...unless you sold your land for a fraction of its previous value and lost your home forever.

Lewis' heart swelled with relief when he glimpsed the familiar tree line. His home waited on the other side. He leapt onto Lila and let her run till they crested the trail and he saw the Dority cabin, the corrals and finally Eldora aboard a well-behaved sorrel. She already had one horse tamed enough to lope a smooth circle around one corral until the horse saw Lewis and Lila approaching and broke stride.

He slowed Lila to a walk.

Eldora did the same with her mount. She sat on the horse beautifully and held the reins at the perfect angle and length. When the sorrel reared, he held his breath, preparing to charge in and put himself between her and the beast should he throw her.

Eldora's soft voice and firm but gentle hand diffused the horse's fear...and his too.

He kept silent and clear, letting her concentrate on her work. He unsaddled Lila, brushed her down, and set her free in the big corral with the other horses. The mare deserved a much greater reward. Considering the amount of riding he'd done lately and might do in the near future, the best thing he could do for her was get another horse saddle-ready.

He scanned his herd, avoided the Appaloosa, and set his attention on a gray gelding.

In neighboring corrals, he and Eldora worked with their chosen mounts. Only the thought of falling behind in the training kept his focus on his horse and not on Eldora.

Until her voice came, soft and sweet and surprisingly near. "I hate to interrupt, but...how was your family? Were they well?"

Glancing over his shoulder, he found her sitting on the top rail, studying him while worrying the end of a slender shoot of spring grass with her teeth. How long had she been watching him?

"They're good." He shortened the lead on the gray and drew him in, praising him in a soft litany until he could stroke his neck as well.

"And Noah and his wife?" The concern tightening her voice rendered him speechless.

Why did she care so much about people she'd never met?

"Good as well," he finally replied. Minus their water concerns, the memory of how good his friends were made him smile. "They couldn't wait to show me their son Jacob's latest achievements."

Her delighted gasp caressed his ears. "They named him after his uncle. He must be proud as well."

He nodded but kept his face averted, along with his expression. He didn't want to erase her happiness.

"I'm so sorry," she whispered. "I didn't know."

"Know what?"

"That something had happened to Noah's brother."

"What makes you think that?"

"Your entire body went rigid. I'm always causing you pain by dredging up the past. I'm sorry."

"Don't be. You're not responsible. Jacob died on a cattle drive to Dodge City a few years ago. Noah blamed himself. He wasn't at fault either."

"But I imagine Noah felt responsible. After his parents' deaths, he'd have become his brother's sole guardian."

"The Ballantyne boys were never alone. They had Jane's parents and my family. Looking out for each other distracted us all from our losses."

She released a heavy sigh. "It's getting late."

When he glanced her way, he caught her frowning up at the sky before she hurried back to nibbling her blade of grass.

"Where's Calhoun?"

She shrugged. "In town."

"You didn't go with him." That fact nearly made him whoop with joy.

"He agreed that I should stay here." Her words fell from her lips like dead leaves, dry and lifeless. Calhoun's change of heart hadn't made her happy. Why?

Her expression revealed nothing.

"If you weren't married, where would you go?" The

question shot out before he could bury it deep inside him with all the other useless things he could've asked. His next question wasn't much better. "Do you have a family somewhere, waiting for you to come home?"

"The show is my home. Samson and Delilah are my family." Each declaration made her vibrate with certainty, with life.

"Have you ever considered a life beyond the show?"

"No. It's the only place where I can ride every day."

Her answer, another echo of Jane's, pierced his heart. She was married to more than Calhoun. Suddenly he hated Calhoun's show as much as the one that had led to Jane's disappearance. Eldora would vanish from his life just like Jane. She'd promised to stay three weeks, but she could leave tomorrow.

The compulsion to keep her close coiled around him like a vine around a tree. Insidious. Smothering. Aggravatingly familiar. If he didn't learn from the past, he'd only make Eldora leave quicker, and he'd never find Jane.

He blew out a long breath and drew another in with equal patience.

"I made you think of her again." She shook her head. "I can't tell you what you want to know most."

"Yes, you can, because right now I only want to know more about you."

"No, you don't. You're lying."

"Am I?" He turned to face her head on.

Disbelief widened her eyes. "What could you possibly want to hear?"

"Tell me about..." He cast about for a topic that wouldn't spook her or make her sad again.

The gray gelding must have sensed his turmoil. He snorted and pranced, tugging on the end of the rope.

Instinctively his hand rose to stroke the horse's neck again. The action calmed them both.

"Tell me about your first show horse," he said.

"Walleyed Charlie." The name tumbled out with youthful delight. "He carried my father home after they mustered out of the army. Half-blind and completely deaf from too much artillery fire, a crowd of civilians disturbed Charlie as much as a butterfly. When asked to run a straight line or a circle, he did so with military precision. He held our act together until I learned balance."

"How'd you do that?"

"Persistence and practice, like your father said." She pressed her lips tight as if she regretted using Jane's words again, as if she had trouble distinguishing between her memories and Jane's.

"Tell me more." He kept his tone light and encouraging. "Where did you practice?"

"Anywhere and on anything. Like here." Grasping the plank she sat on, she climbed up to crouch atop the fence. Then she let go and rose to stand tall and graceful, like a branch sprouting from a treetop rather than a corral he'd cobbled together with limited resources.

"That's not the sturdiest of perches. Come down and balance on...a rock or something."

Her laughter swirled around him, teasing him with wicked delight. "It's either this plank or the back of a horse."

"Or we could call it a day. Like you said, it's getting late and—"

"Don't worry. I've done this a thousand times."

"Not on that fence. You can't trust my carpentry skills."

"Yes, I can." She bounced on the rail. "See. You can trust me as well. I know what I'm doing." An ominous snap below her feet made her freeze, except for her gaze, which darted downward. Too late.

He reached for her at the same time that the wood split in two. She toppled backward, arms windmilling, struggling to resurrect herself, refusing to accept her fate. A heartbeat later, she curled into a ball and hit the mud by the water trough.

The wet earth splashed everywhere as she rolled. He vaulted over the fence, trying to reach her. When he finally did, she lay unnaturally still—except for the tremors shaking her shoulders.

How badly was she hurt? Juniper Flats didn't have a doctor. It'd take hours of jarring riding to carry her to the next town and find the care she might require. He'd have to cause her more pain before he could help her.

The dire thought sent him crashing to his knees beside her. "What did you hurt?"

She burst into laughter. Or rather, let loose the laughter that he realized she'd been trying to hold on to. "You mean besides your fence? Nothing, as long as we don't count my pride." She rolled onto her back with arms and legs splayed wide.

Relief left him limp as a rag doll, but also grinning. "No more practicing today."

"Agreed. I haven't fallen like that in years. Falling is inevitable. But falling while ignoring good advice and while bragging..." She groaned and covered her muddy face with her even muddier hands. "I'm a complete fool."

"Never." Now that he knew she was uninjured, he wanted only to hear her laugh again. "A complete fool wouldn't have the sense to land on the only soft ground around. You've a rare talent for finding a mud puddle."

Her groan deepened. "I must look frightful."

She looked damned good lying so close to him. Except with her hands still covering her face, he couldn't see her eyes. *Look at me, Angel Eyes.* "To me, you look perfect."

"Now I know you're lying."

"I'm glad you fell in the mud."

Finally, she lowered her hands and pushed up on her elbows to stare at him, eyes dancing with curiosity. "That's an odd thing to be glad about. Me, I'd be happier if I hadn't fallen."

"Falling is inevitable," he reminded her.

As the lines around her eyes crinkled with pleasure, her irises took on a radiant copper tone, scorching him with their warmth.

His heart pounded with anticipation. Any second now he'd hear her laughter. "As long as you're not hurt, I'm happy. But next time..."

"Yes?" She leaned closer.

He did the same. "You could try falling my way."

"You'd catch me?" Her gasp of pure pleasure was reflected in her eyes. "What if I stood on the fence again and jumped? We could practice that tomorrow."

"No," the word shot out gruffer than he intended. "We shouldn't." *You need to stay safe.* "No more playing the daredevil."

Her shoulders slumped with defeat. The sight made his spirits droop as well. He'd done the last thing he wanted to do. He'd smothered her happiness.

"You see me only as a thrill seeker, and maybe I am. But a life without leaping means..."

"No falling."

"And no soaring...or catching." She frowned at her muddy hands.

"No getting dirty."

"And no enjoying a bath afterward." A faint smile tugged her lips. "Up here in the wilderness, I don't suppose there's a place where I can have one?"

"You're sitting right next to your bathtub." The urge to turn her glum smile into a happy one, to bring her close again, made him scoop her up in his arms. He was rewarded with her shriek of laughter. His happiness soared with the sound of hers. "*Up here*—" He lifted her higher, and the sweet music of her laughter rose as well. "If you don't include our rivers and creeks, your bathtub is the water trough. And knowing you, you'll want to jump in fast." He held her over the trough, then dipped low, pretending to drop her in.

One glance at the water and her face went white as frost on a clear winter night. She twined her arms around his neck and hid against his chest. This time the trembling in her body was all fear.

He held her tight as well. "What's wrong?"

She lifted her head enough to stare at him with eyes drowning in dark memories. "I'm being foolish again. The trough isn't deep, but it reminds me of—" She shook her head and pressed her face to his chest again.

"The steamboat sinking on the Mississippi." He spun away from the water and set her on her feet by the corral. "Hold on to this." He wrapped her hands around a post. The faraway look clouding her eyes made him squeeze her hand just hard enough to bring her focus back to him. "Hold on to this strong and reliable fence I built"—he winked at her —"while I fetch something from the cabin. I'll be right back."

He returned carrying a chair and a bowl. "Do you trust me?

She nodded without hesitation.

"Then have a seat, and I'll bring your bath to you. One bowl at a time."

The first bowl he held in front of her while she sat and splashed the water on her face. When she raised her head and smiled at him, the water sparkled on her lashes and lips like morning dew. His mouth grew parched, begging him to lean down and take a sip.

He busied himself with the task of bringing her more water. When he held the bowl over her head, he paused. "Tilt your head back as far as you can." He doubted the steadiness of his hands when she did as asked and gazed up at him like a lover still waiting for her kiss. "Better close your eyes as well."

When she did as he suggested, he poured the water with infinite care, slowly, gently over her head. The coldness made her lips part on a hushed gasp.

His steps dragged as he went to retrieve another bowl of water. When he returned, he plucked the yellow ribbon from the end of her braid and tucked it in his pocket for safekeeping. This time when he poured, he combed his fingers through her hair, uncoiling her braid in order to coax out the remaining mud.

The silky wet strands slipped tantalizingly through his fingers until his hand found a home cradling the back of her head. He held her close, mesmerized by her lips parting wider and wider with each ragged breath. Then her lashes flickered and her eyes opened, and time stopped.

Until her shiver shook him from his trance.

He glanced around them, at the shadows that had arrived out of nowhere. When had the sun dipped below the horizon and taken the day with it?

Eldora shivered again. He released her and the bowl. He focused on unbuttoning his shirt as fast as his fumbling fingers would go. Her eyes flared impossibly wide, but she didn't utter a sound. He shrugged out of his shirt and draped it around her shoulders to keep her clean hair away from her muddy clothing. Then he grasped her hand and pulled her to her feet.

She came to rest a whisper away from his naked chest, staring up at him with the same expression as when he'd shielded her from Calhoun and his horse. One wish thudded in his head and formed a silent plea: *Stay with me, Angel Eyes.*

A frown puckered her brow.

"Don't worry," he said. "You're safe with me."

"I know."

"Then why do you continue to look worried?"

"Not worried, but..." A dazzling smile curved her lips and crinkled the lines around her eyes.

His heart raced, sending his blood surging south of his belt buckle.

"It's my turn to be stunned." Her whispered words and soft sigh tickled his chest and stoked the lust roaring inside him. Before he could pull her snug against him, she said, "No one's ever called me anything as beautiful as Angel Eyes before."

Disbelief froze him. He'd actually said the name out loud? Damn his loose lips and his futile fascination for a woman who could never be his to hold. She was married to another man.

He released her abruptly and bent to retrieve the bowl and hide his face. Maybe his adoration wasn't as easy to read as his lies. Maybe they could go back to working the horses together. Maybe he could keep her by his side even if he couldn't hold her in his arms.

"Lewis..."

The silence that followed the glorious sound of his name on her lips shredded his nerves. His hopes were about to go up in smoke.

"I wish I could tell you I'm not married, but I can't." Her confession wrapped around him like a bittersweet embrace. She desired him as well. And they both knew it was wrong.

He cleared his throat, battling the misery that rumbled in the sound and inside him. "Your muddy clothing must be cold and uncomfortable. Do you have something else to wear?"

"Roy brought my travel case from town yesterday. It's inside the cabin."

"Better go in then and change before you catch a chill. I'll build a fire over there." He pointed to the fire pit enclosed by rocks on the other side of the cabin.

When she didn't move, he snuck a peek at her. She stared at the cabin with an expression so full of uncertainty it held room for nothing else.

He searched for a way to ease her concerns. "If you like, I can heat up some stew I made the other day. I warn you I'm about as good a cook as I am a carpenter, but it might be edible with the help of the biscuits Sadie gave me." He turned his back to her and the temptation of watching her enter his home, or even worse, following her inside.

The minutes she was gone sorely tested his willpower. He welcomed the distraction of building the fire. When the door squeaked open, he couldn't help but glance over his shoulder. Then he stopped breathing.

The firelight made her pale pink dress glow soft and warm, while her still-damp hair hung long and loose over the wool shawl around her shoulders. He'd expected her to come out in another tailored outfit, like the one she'd arrived in. The simplicity of her new garments made her look like a humble homesteader's wife. The sight definitely humbled him.

He wanted to jump up and carry her back inside the cabin and—

She handed him a clean shirt. "Thought you might be cold as well."

He felt like his skin was on fire when she ran her gaze over him. Only when she crossed to collect the chair and set it by the fire pit did he finally remember the shirt in his hands and put it on.

She sat and used a horse brush to scrub the mud from her boots. The white of her chemise flashed beckoningly under the hem of her skirt, drawing his gaze up her ankle and then the curve of her calf—which shivered along with the rest of her.

His gaze jumped to her face, pale and drawn. "You're still cold."

She met his gaze briefly, then continued cleaning her boots. An apologetic smile hovered on her lips. "I didn't pack sensibly for this trip." She gestured to the rocks and trees around them. "I didn't anticipate living in the wilderness. Residing in hotel suites and private railcars has dulled my strength."

There was nothing dull or weak about her. She was only chilled and wearing inadequate clothing.

He stood in a rush. "I've something else for you inside the cabin." He retrieved his winter jacket and a pair of wool socks. "They're not much, but they're yours if you want them."

She nodded and accepted his meager offerings like they were the richest of garments. As she slipped into his jacket, she paused to rub her cheek against the soft fleece collar. When she caught him staring, she focused on trading her wet but no longer muddy boots for his thick socks. His clothing swallowed her up, but didn't hide the blush on her cheeks.

He'd called her perfect, covered in mud. He'd meant it. But she looked a hundred times better bundled up in his clothes.

"Thank you for showing me such generosity. Especially after I came here and—" She drew his coat tighter around her. "Every story I heard about you is true. You're a good friend."

"No, I'm not."

"Yes, you are. You should, however, do something about your stubborn streak."

Her gentle teasing went to his head like a shot of fine whiskey. "If I should, then so should you. Or we could call ourselves determined and stay as we are."

"You sound like...someone I left behind with the show." Her expression turned pinched and pensive. "Whatever word we use, I imagine one needs a lot of it to thrive in the wilderness. Don't you ever get lonely up here?"

"Not often. And Juniper Flats isn't that far away."

"Too far for some to travel." She glanced at the trail that led to town, and to her husband and his guard.

"Did Calhoun say when he'd return?" He hoped she'd say never.

"Before nightfall."

"Why did you marry him?" He immediately regretted his question. There could be no good answers. He wanted her to say she wasn't married. Only an idiot wished for the impossible.

"After the steamboat accident, I needed—" She clutched his jacket in a white-knuckled grip, as if it were a lifeline. "I don't know. I felt adrift, lost. Roy provided an anchor. He was different back then. Maybe I was as well. We bonded over working together to make the show the best in the country."

"He married you to ensure you never left his show."

Her breath hissed in her throat, and he cursed his careless words.

"I'm sorry. I shouldn't have said that."

"Why not?" She shrugged one shoulder. "It's true."

"It's not the only reason he married you. Whatever the case, you deserve more. What I wanted to say was—" He swallowed the words. He couldn't stop them from pounding in his head and his heart.

*I want to be the one to give you more. Don't go back to Calhoun. Stay with me.*

She stared at him with a puzzled look. Heaven help him, had he said his thoughts aloud again? He prayed for a miracle.

"What did you want to say?" she asked.

He drew in a deep breath and chose his reply carefully. "I've...learned nothing in eighteen years. My hasty words, my self-centered thoughts...drove Jane away as well."

"On that subject you're wrong."

The certainty in her voice startled him. "You weren't there. How do you know?"

"I just do." Her gaze rose to the sky, to the stars starting to sparkle against the deepening indigo blanket high above them. "I know something else. Roy isn't coming back tonight."

*I hope he never comes back.* His mind was tumbling once again into a dangerous land filled with futile hopes. Calhoun should never have left her alone with him nearby.

"He'll return when it suits him," she said. "Until then, I'm on my own."

"No. You're not. I'll be sleeping outside by the fire."

She frowned. "That sounds cold and uncomfortable."

He strove to make light of the arrangement. "I've bedded down in worse. Torrential downpours. Freezing blizzards. Several crude camp towns and equally unsavory cities. Like Dodge. Couldn't wait to leave that hellhole." He gritted his teeth to stop his rambling. Nothing could stop his rising excitement about sleeping a handful of strides away from Eldora, or closer.

"You could...stay inside the cabin."

His mouth went dry as dirt. He'd never get a second of sleep if he went inside with her. "I'll be fine out here."

"Well, if you wake up tired and cranky, don't be surprised if tomorrow I pull even further ahead in our wager." She picked up her boots and began scrubbing them again, this time with short, agitated strokes.

*Damn the wager, Angel Eyes. I want to work with you, not against you.* "The sorrel came along nicely. You did a good job with him."

She shrugged and continued cleaning her boots, even though they no longer needed it. "I did no better than you did with the gray."

Why was she lying to him and belittling her talent? "I didn't get beyond putting a lead rope on him. Today you won our bet."

Her expression had become closed, her thoughts impossible to read. "It wasn't a fair contest. I had a head start."

He heaved a sigh of resignation. "Tomorrow you'll have another." Maybe tomorrow he could find a way to bring her closer again. But first, he'd have to leave her for a couple of hours. He wished she could come with him, but it wouldn't be safe. Not with a mountain lion and possibly more sinkholes out there. He had to stop obsessing about what he wanted and instead do what was best for Eldora.

She halted her scrubbing, but her gaze remained on her boots. "What happens tomorrow?"

"I'm riding out early to check the highland."

"For what?"

"My trough and cistern might hold water, but Sadie told me their creeks were dry. Their water comes from the highland."

"The townsfolk were lamenting a lack of spring rains when we passed through."

"That doesn't help." But it wasn't the whole answer. "Over the years, the headwaters have chosen their own paths and destinations. Destinations every homesteader and rancher have come to depend upon. One branch comes this way, several others to the Ballantyne Ranch, more partner up to form the river feeding Juniper Flats. Water is the lifeblood of this country."

She nodded. "If it's diverted or goes underground..." She swallowed hard.

"Don't worry. Sinkholes aren't common."

"And mountain lions?"

"Even less so."

She finally turned to look at him. Her mask was gone. Concern furrowed her brow and tightened her lips. "How long will you be gone?"

*Too long.* He'd be lucky if he could even leave without looking back a hundred times. That would slow him down. "Can't really say, but I'll be back." No force on earth could stop him from doing that.

"I should come with you."

He fought the urge to agree. Too many dangers lurked in

the hills for him to be selfish and agree to her riding by his side again. "You should stay at the homestead."

"But—"

"It's not open for discussion."

Her eyes widened with disbelief. "That statement is a thousand miles from you saying you wouldn't tell me what to do yesterday."

"Maybe so. But I also said your safety, and Jane's, was my first priority. So what I'm saying now is you'll be safer staying behind."

"You're saying whatever partnership we had is over." She dropped her scrub brush and leapt to her feet. "Fine. I have more important things to do tomorrow."

He racked his brain for a peace offering, a way to coax her to sit down again and stay with him a while longer. "Shall I bring out that stew I mentioned? And the biscuits? You must be hungry."

"I'm not. I'm..." She spun toward the cabin. "I'm tired. I'm going to sleep, because then tomorrow will come faster. I have a lot to do. Alone." She walked away from him with swift strides, almost running. "Goodbye, Mr. Adams."

# CHAPTER 5

*K*eeping one hand on Samson's reins and the other on Lewis' handgun strapped to her hip, Eldora scanned the trees and their many shadows. No tawny eyes stared back, no limping gait rustled the under-brush, no mountain lion leapt out with flashing teeth and claws. Nevertheless, she struggled not to turn back, back to the Dority homestead and Lewis.

No use going back. Lewis had left before daybreak, as he said he would. She'd stood by the window and watched him go. She'd hoped that he'd turn back. That he'd ask her to go with him. That he wanted her by his side.

When she'd first arrived, she'd hoped they could work together for Jane's sake. Then she'd hoped for a whole lot more.

She'd rolled the dice. Taken a chance. And lost. Their brief partnership had ended as abruptly as it had started. Her longstanding one with Roy was over as well.

She was truly alone, with worries multiplying by the minute.

Why hadn't Roy returned yesterday as promised?

Knowing him, he'd only promised to get what he wanted most. He hadn't wanted her to stay at the Dority homestead. But after talking to Hawk, he hadn't demanded or even asked if she'd reconsider and accompany him back to town.

Roy didn't want her in Juniper Flats. So that was where she must go.

She must also return to the homestead before Lewis did. If she didn't, he'd ask questions. Questions she didn't want to answer.

She should've gone at night when Lewis, Roy, Vandrill, and Juniper Flats' townsfolk were asleep, or more likely to be. She hadn't slept much last night. Not imagining Lewis lying on his bedroll outside the cabin. Too far away, but also too close.

He was a distraction she couldn't afford. But even if he hadn't camped outside the cabin and kept watch over her for the night, she still wouldn't have risked riding Samson in the dark over unfamiliar terrain.

No matter what some people thought—including one very opinionated Texan—she was not a senseless daredevil. Samson, though strong and willing, was still recovering from a nightmare past with Buckley's Circus. Outside the familiar routine of the show, that past occasionally rendered him flighty and his own worst enemy.

Delilah, on the other hand, though she might not be as grand in appearance, was as dependable as the sun rising. As the land gradually changed from forest to fields, the speck that was Juniper Flats grew, along with her worries.

The town had changed since she'd seen it two days ago. A traveling show camped on its edge. A show with many familiar tents and wagons. A show that should've been two towns and three river crossings away. This was why Roy hadn't wanted her to talk to Hawk yesterday. Roy had agreed that the show shouldn't come to Juniper Flats. So why was it now here?

Hurrying down the back streets, she took Samson to the livery and paid the sleepy stable boy to keep him there. Then she paid the boy again, this time to keep quiet about Samson and her being in town.

Another string of deserted alleys allowed her to approach the show unseen. Or so she hoped.

She sprinted across the stretch of open field to reach the one caravan that stood out from the rest like a faded relic from a bygone era. Its curtains remained closed. Not a sound came from inside.

With equally silent hands and feet, she climbed its six-rung stepladder, opened its door, and entered its shadowy interior. The muzzle of a shotgun protruding from the dark stopped her.

"Sorry, Peanut." The words came low and rasping, like a blacksmith's file. "Hoped it might be you. Couldn't risk being wrong."

The gun retreated into the gloom. A match flared, illuminating a gnarled hand reaching for an oil lantern.

She jerked the door closed behind her and prayed no one would see the light. Then she faced the old man perched like a stork on the foot of the unmade bed that filled most of the tiny interior. With broad strokes, he smoothed the sheets, then his rumpled suit and wild white hair. He made a big production of it. Too big.

A person new to the art of distraction did that when trying to conceal something. Gaylon was too experienced a showman to make that mistake...unless he was overwhelmed by his own distractions.

"Why did Roy bring the show here? Why did you let him? Has anyone recognized you? What about Jane? I mean

Dory." Worry made her questions tumble out, leaving her breathless.

He raised his palms. "Whoa there, Peanut! I'm excited to see you as well, but you better slow down before you fall down."

There wasn't time. A single sideways step kept her upright as she leaned against the caravan wall. "You shouldn't be here."

"Neither should you."

She nudged the window curtain aside and peered out. The camp remained the way she'd found it. Quiet as the lull before a storm. She kept looking. "How much time do we have?"

"Before Roy finds you with me? Probably not enough. You—" A rattling cough made him pause. Not for long, but long enough to spike her worry. His next words didn't help. "You should've told me about the blackmailer."

She clutched the curtain tight. "I didn't want to worry Jane."

"Or me."

She sealed her lips against the need to ask about his health. That would only lead to more teasing or worse, silence. Gaylon had always been the caregiver—to her and everyone around him. Fanatically so. Like he was making up for a grave sin. He'd been this way even before Juniper Flats.

Worry and a lack of sleep weakened her legs and sent her sliding down the wall. The stool he always kept at the foot of his bed caught her.

How many had sat here and shared both concerns and complaints with Gaylon since he'd agreed to merge his show with Roy's and become just another wheel keeping Roy's life rolling? All to help Eldora and Jane achieve their desire to entertain larger audiences.

Gaylon had given up his freedom running his own show in order to make them happy and remain in their lives. A life where guests came and went with the rising and setting of the sun, and performers who became family came and went with the seasons.

She didn't want to lose Gaylon or Jane. But she must do what was best for them, not for her. She had to get Gaylon away from Juniper Flats before someone recognized him. Unfortunately, her knees were shaking so badly that she couldn't even rise from her seat.

"The sins from this town are mine," Gaylon said with a sigh. "Not yours."

"You're as stubborn as an old goat."

He released a gravelly chuckle. "I prefer to call myself tenacious." Gaylon always had.

Yesterday Lewis had called himself determined. Today she needed something else.

"Be honest." She stared at her knees and willed them to stop shaking. "We share the blame. We both encouraged Jane to stay with us. We should've taken her back immediately."

"We're back now, and it's not like you to hide from me. Look at me. Be honest with me as well."

She couldn't do either. "I'm sorry I didn't tell you about the blackmailer."

"What about Jane's friend?"

"Lewis? What about him?"

"You always wanted to meet him. Now you have, but you're not telling me about him either."

"He's just as she described." Except he was tall and sinfully distracting and a hundred times better than the dream man she'd built in her head. "He never forgot Jane. He'll help her."

"And you, too."

"He shouldn't. I only came to take his home."

"Looks like you took his coat instead," Gaylon said, running his gaze over her.

"This isn't a joking matter." This morning she'd convinced herself she needed his coat's comfort as much as his revolver's protection. Neither item was easing her current distress. Her hands were shaking as badly as her legs now. She grabbed her knees and held on tight.

Gaylon laid his hands over hers and squeezed gently. His rasping cough returned. It filled the room and didn't stop.

Fear sent her heart thudding in her chest. "Where's your flask?"

"Don't—need it—anymore."

"Now isn't the time to stop drinking when it can ease your cough."

"That's—not—why I—"

"Stop arguing. If you won't drink, then do as you always advised me. Concentrate on breathing. Ignore the rest for the moment."

"Good—advice," he wheezed. "You do—the same."

After a long moment, his coughing ceased, and so did her shaking. Even sick, he was her rock. She was no longer alone. Gaylon was with her, as he'd been every day of her life until she'd left him to steal the Dority homestead.

"Peanut, you came for his land. And land isn't everything."

She tried to pull away from him and his words. He held tight. Goats were strong as well as stubborn and tenacious until time caught up with them. She bit back her sob.

He patted her hand. "Land doesn't make a home. Neither does a show. People do."

"You have to leave."

"I'll never leave you."

"But you cannot stay. What if someone remembers you?" In his current condition, he wouldn't last long if the authorities locked him in a dank jail cell.

"It's worth the gamble. Besides, I'm wagering eighteen years will erase all but the most stalwart of memories. Did anyone recognize you?"

Her throat tightened with disappointment.

"I'm sorry, Peanut."

"Don't be. I didn't expect Lewis to remember me."

"You're all grown up. You're a far cry from that young girl."

"But you still call me Peanut."

"Because that's what you are and have always been. Peanuts are important. Despite their size, they make a show thrive."

Silence filled the room while one useless question filled her mind. Why didn't Lewis remember her?

"Why is it so important that he remembers?" Gaylon asked.

"Because I remembered him." Her voice sounded needy, like a child's whine. She scrunched up her nose in disgust.

"You watched him watching our show, but afterward you had Jane's stories to keep him alive in your memories and in your heart. And I watched you fall in love with a stranger, day by day."

She forced her face to relax and assume a well-practiced blank mask. This wasn't the time to dwell in the past. "None of that matters now. Only the blackmailer matters. What did Roy tell you about him?"

"Nothing."

"Roy's already shut me out. Don't do the same."

"I'm not. And we don't need Roy. We've got Vandrill. He's keeping me informed."

Surprise sharpened her voice. "Vandrill? We can't trust him. He works for Roy."

"So do we."

She blew out a long breath, trying to release her agitation, so she could think. "What if Roy asked Vandrill to feed us false information to test our loyalty?"

"That's a possibility. But Vandrill is more than he appears. He has his own agenda."

"Which is?"

"He didn't share that part." He raised his palms again, stopping the frustrated remark hovering on her tongue. "And I didn't ask. I want him to continue sharing what he learns."

"What has he told you?"

"That Roy had received anonymous letters demanding the Dority homestead. That Roy hadn't told you everything. That you didn't know about—" He ran his hands over the rumpled bedsheets on either side of him, this time with frantic, needy strokes.

She'd always assumed he'd started drinking because of his illness. But he wasn't coughing now. She glimpsed a flash of silver, retrieved the flask and pressed it into his hands, which trembled worse than hers had a moment before. "What don't I know?"

Gaylon took a long swig of whiskey. "Why Roy brought you here."

"We're here to keep a blackmailer from telling the world that certain members of a Wild West show with a previously spotless reputation once practiced child theft."

"That's one reason."

"There's another?"

Gaylon raised the flask to his lips again, but halted short. "This reason is more important to Roy than to me." He lowered the flask. "You girls are everything to me. Vandrill said the blackmailer knew why I'd left the army twenty-four years ago."

"That's no secret. The army granted you a discharge for bravery in battle."

"Their words, not mine. I was merely a parrot repeating them."

The resignation and sadness in his voice made her chest tighten with dread. "What— What did you do?"

"I did as ordered. We murdered innocents."

*Murder.* The word sucked the air from the room. *Just concentrate on breathing. Ignore the rest for the moment.*

"It's time for the truth, for that honesty you wanted." His words sounded far away, but they still yanked her back to a truth she didn't want to face. She couldn't imagine Gaylon killing or even hurting anyone, but he'd been in the army, and he hadn't been a cook or a clerk.

*We murdered innocents.*

"You said *we*. Who is—?" Another truth fell into place and constricted her throat as the name came with it. "Roy."

Gaylon nodded. "It gets worse."

Only one way it could. "You're talking about the fabled battle that started Roy's career."

"He can't allow his version of heroic glory to be shattered. He's not trying to cover up our past in Juniper Flats" —he gestured between the two of them—"as much as his and mine in Nebraska. That's what Vandrill told me."

"No." She lurched to her feet and paced in a tight circle. The cramped space wouldn't allow more. The walls pressed in. "Vandrill may be Roy's guard and lawyer, but Roy wouldn't share any of this with him or anyone."

"He didn't. Same as with you, he showed Vandrill only one letter. Afterward, Vandrill went through Roy's belongings and found a second."

"Why did he do that?" Why hadn't she done that?

"A man named Smith urged him to search for more letters. Apparently, this Smith fellow feels the blackmailer committed a crime equal to mine and Roy's. He's trying to collect the necessary evidence."

"Is he a blackmailer as well?"

"Vandrill suspected he was a lawman."

The law getting involved would be a disaster. She prayed it wasn't true. What if it wasn't? "What if there's no Smith? What if Vandrill is the blackmailer?"

"The blackmailer knew details that could only be gained by witnessing the battle in Nebraska. How the settlers accused the Sioux of stealing a cow and demanded compensation. How we marched out to the reservation to find only starving women and children with their men gone to find food. How Roy ordered a retreat that never happened."

"Why not?"

"Roy was young and arrogant, fresh out of West Point. The men wouldn't listen to him. They wanted to take a Sioux woman. When that didn't work out, they started shooting."

"But you didn't."

He shook his head. "Neither did Roy. But we couldn't stop the soldiers, and when it was over, all Roy complained about was his career being over as well. The soldiers said he had bigger worries, like what would happen when the hunters came back and found their families dead."

They would have gone on the warpath. She would have. "What did Roy do?"

"He led us out to hunt the hunters, to catch them by

surprise, to kill them before they killed us. Then he ordered all the bodies, both white and native, hauled back to the reservation and oversaw their strategic placement."

The horror of that battlefield flashed in her mind like still images from a tragic stage play. Warriors locked in combat. Women clutching weapons...and their children.

"He staged his first show," she whispered.

"Then he encouraged what remained of his men to have a celebratory drink. I was contemplating desertion when he pressed a gun against my back and another into my hand. We returned to the fort, the only survivors. Roy became a hero and expedited my discharge papers. I went free of the army."

She shook her head. "But never free of the past or Roy. When he learned about the Eldorado Jane act, he used that past to make you join him again."

"Makes me wonder what he's done to persuade others to perform in his show."

"Vandrill is deadly accurate with his Winchester. He plays the soldier to perfection when he swaps that rifle for his Sharps cavalry carbine. It's like he's not even acting. Could he have been at the battle?"

"No. Twenty-four years ago he would've been a child. No children with his pale coloring were there that day." Gaylon swallowed hard and took another gulp from his flask.

His previous words wormed their way into her thoughts again: *We murdered innocents.*

"You didn't shoot them."

"I didn't save them either. But there was....a half-breed boy with a very pretty Sioux mother. The soldiers called her a whore who should return to her duties at the fort. The boy pulled a knife. They took it from him. Said he needed to be taught a lesson. That's when it started: the running, the screaming, the shooting." He stared at the flask in his hand, as if seeing the past there. "Only that boy lived, half-hidden under his mother's body, his face a bloody mess of cuts. That was the soldiers' lesson."

"You saw him?"

"Not for long. The devastation carved upon his face and reflected in his eyes was unbearable. So I looked the other way. I made sure Roy did the same."

The faces of all the natives who'd previously worked in the show—plus the dozen, including Hawk, currently traveling with them—flashed through her mind. She'd assumed they were men eager to earn funds for their families, or adventurers seeking excitement. She'd hoped that eventually, if not friends, they'd become at least allies.

Any one of them could be that ruined boy grown into a vengeful man, a blackmailer with a grim reason to exact revenge. But none of them had a scarred face.

"He may've healed without scars," Gaylon said.

"But why demand the Dority's land? Why not money?"

"Hell if I know. And I can't see that boy in any of the men sleeping out there." He gestured to the show camp outside the caravan.

Soon those men and Roy would be waking. Soon Lewis would return to the homestead. Soon she must return as well. The land held answers. But if she left, who'd keep Gaylon safe? Certainly not Roy. And despite Gaylon's belief in Vandrill, she still couldn't trust him.

Her world had become a storm of unanswerable questions and shadowy enemies. Only one person could help her now. She glanced over her shoulder, preparing to head for the door. "I need Jane."

"Sorry, Peanut. You won't find her here." He drained the

contents of the flask. "Not in her wagon or anywhere in the camp."

*I will never return home now.* The memory of Jane's vow following the sinking of a steamboat brought her to her knees beside Gaylon.

She grabbed his hand as they reached for each other. "She's left us."

STANDING beside the last building on the eastern edge of Juniper Flats, Lewis read the elaborate script on the poster nailed to its clapboard wall: *Colonel Calhoun's Wondrous West.*

The warm velvet of Eldora's yellow ribbon clutched in his hand provided little comfort as his gaze swept down to the annoyingly accurate drawing of Calhoun's arrogant face before settling on Eldora standing atop Samson—being chased at full gallop by soldiers brandishing bayonets, natives with bows and arrows, and a variety of other determined-looking pursuers, including the buffalo she'd mentioned.

Was she a self-centered thrill seeker who lived only for the crowd? An actress who'd played him with pretty words and promises? Whatever she'd done yesterday, she'd abandoned the Dority homestead and him today. She'd left as soon as she could. The moment he'd ridden out to check the headwaters.

Luckily, he'd turned back. He'd been unable to leave her, which was a feeling she obviously didn't return. He'd followed her at a distance, wanting to keep her safe and learn where she needed to go so badly she'd ridden out in the gloom of predawn.

When he realized she was heading to town, his heart

had hurt that she couldn't embrace the seclusion of his home. Then he'd seen the show camped on the outskirts. His pain had doubled.

How had she known her show was here? Had she lied to him, and it'd been here all the time? Or had Calhoun and his guard told her yesterday? If that were the case, then why hadn't she gone with them?

She'd said Calhoun agreed she should stay behind. Maybe she hadn't known the show was here, but had suspected. Maybe he wasn't the only one being outmaneuvered and left in the dust. Or, more likely, he just wanted to believe in a less deceitful version of Eldora.

She could very well be his downfall, like Delilah had been Samson's.

In all his life, he'd only seen one other traveling show. *Gypson's Medicine Show*. Eighteen years ago. Here in Juniper Flats. With Jane Dority by his side.

Jane wasn't here now. All because of a show—and him.

He shoved Eldora's ribbon deep in his pocket and ripped the poster from the wall. He crumpled the paper into a ball, squeezing so hard his hand ached as he scanned the tents and wagons sprawling in the field like a slumbering giant—foreboding and foreign but also serene in the hush of dawn. Until the damned monstrosity woke up and started gobbling up more of his life.

He resumed his watch over the tiny caravan that had swallowed Eldora and now wouldn't spit her out. Its faded murals swirled like pastel ghosts around the door and window that, no matter how closely he stared, remained still and eerily dark. Only the caravan's brightly painted sign moved, swaying in the breeze, but not enough to blur its crisp red letters forming the words *Show Office*.

A sudden gust of wind sent an icy chill down the back of

his collar. The narrow stretch of earth between him and the caravan kicked up a cloud of dust, messing with his view of the office. Except for the sign which rocked like a child's swing, building speed and creaking with taunting laughter.

To hell with waiting, playing it safe, and accepting that he might lose Eldora today. She'd promised to stay for three weeks. She'd enjoyed training his horses with him. She'd wanted to kiss him.

It was high time she came out of that caravan and told him everything she knew about Jane. He didn't care if Calhoun found out. He wasn't waiting.

He was getting Jane back, and Eldora too.

Every step closer to the caravan deepened his feeling that its birth predated its sign and the rest of the show by a decade or maybe two. The neighboring wagons shone with fresh paint and spotless brass. The tents rippled with crisp pennants and colorful fabrics. The largest tent towered like a castle in a child's storybook, its striped peak higher than Juniper Flats' tallest building.

The smaller print on the caravan's sign became visible: *All Inquiries Welcome.*

He huffed in incredulity. Not likely. At least not the inquiries he had.

An overwhelming sense of familiarity buffeted him, till a grim certainty slammed him to a halt at the foot of the stepladder leading to a door to the past. This caravan had once belonged to *Gypson's Medicine Show.*

He jammed the poster into the pocket containing Eldora's ribbon and raised his rifle. He took the half-dozen steps in two strides. Yanked open the door.

Inside, Eldora knelt beside an old man. Thin and frail. Scruffy as a tramp. She clutched his hand as if he was a king she worshiped.

"Welcome back to the show, son," the man said in a hoarse but still-strong voice. The same voice that had enticed visitors closer and introduced them to an acrobatic rider, while touting an elixir that would cure all your woes.

"Gypson," he growled, leveling his rifle at the man. "Your show ends here. Tell me where Jane is, or I'll—"

Lightning fast, Eldora jumped between them. "You'll have to shoot me before I let you harm my father."

# CHAPTER 6

"*Y*ou should call me father more often," Gaylon said wistfully.

Eldora ignored him and kept her gaze on Lewis. His thumb hovered over the hammer, ready to cock the rifle. Anger radiated from his body, scorching her with his fiery condemnation.

"Reminds me of when you were little," Gaylon added. "When I started calling you Peanut."

"Gaylon," she said in a warning tone. "You're not helping."

"If he's your father, then you're—" Lewis lowered his rifle as shock and then disbelief raced across his features. "You're that girl whose routine we mimicked."

She stiffened. *That girl.* The two words crackled with criticism.

"And you're blind, Adams," Gaylon shot back in her defense.

"Gaylon, please be quiet."

"Not only blind," Gaylon huffed, "but self-absorbed to have taken so long to remember her."

Lewis lunged forward to glare over her shoulder at Gaylon. "And you're a royal jackass not to take your daughter's advice and shut the hell up. I remember you both now." He stabbed his finger at Gaylon. "You brought your Medicine Show to my home, peddling a potion that would solve all our problems. You left and my best friend vanished that same night. If you hurt her, I'll—" He reached around her to grab Gaylon.

Eldora seized his arm and twisted. Pain shot across his features as his gaze locked with hers. He didn't fight her grasp or try to pull away. He accepted the pain. His pain became hers, deep in her heart. Lewis thought he deserved this hurt.

She loosened her grip but didn't let go. "Jane came with us willingly." She concentrated on making her voice as soothing as possible. "You remember her. She said she wanted to ride all day and night."

Lewis jerked back, and she let him go. He stood, breathing heavily, shaking with too many emotions to name.

"We welcomed her into our family," Gaylon said. "I loved her like a daughter."

Lewis' glare found Gaylon again. "You robbed her real family of eighteen years of loving her." His gaze jumped back to her. "And you? Are you his real daughter, or did he steal you from some family as well?"

Silence filled the caravan. Gaylon did not contradict him. *No, it couldn't be true. He would've told me. I would've known.*

"Peanut!" Gaylon's shout echoed off the walls. Then from farther away came the command, "Grab her before she falls."

Lewis held her close as the light that made up her world

dimmed. "I shouldn't have said that," he whispered against her ear. "It isn't true."

Behind her, the bed squeaked, and the room filled with a massive coughing fit.

A flash of pure fear startled her back to life. She shoved away from Lewis and stumbled to the bed where Gaylon lay curled in a ball, coughing like he might splinter into a thousand pieces. She grasped his shaking shoulder and held on tight. "Just breathe."

"I'd rather—he—shot me."

"Stop teasing," she begged.

"I'm not."

"Then stop being so stubborn. I'm not going to let you die!"

Gaylon's coughing subsided, replaced by a litany of words so low she had to lean closer to hear. "I deserve to be punished for the future I stole from Jane, and from you and your mother. I left her for the army. When I finally returned, she had a baby, and a year left to live. I'm not your—"

"You'll *always* be my father."

"I love both you and Jane. You're the daughters of my heart. I won't let you suffer for my crimes."

"We've all made mistakes."

"You're not a murderer."

Lewis' horrified gasp shot over her shoulder. "Who did he kill?"

"Not Jane. He's talking about his time in the army. Long before we met Jane outside Juniper Flats."

The heat of Lewis' body came closer, simmering with questions. She couldn't bear to look at him and see the anger that must blaze in his eyes.

She waited for him to speak, but he didn't. So she did. "We were hunkered down in this caravan, staring out the window at God's fury and magnificence when Jane rode out of the storm, standing on her horse. She said she'd come to join our show. We said it'd be wrong to leave without telling anyone. We'd take her home so she could talk to her family."

"But you didn't."

"She wouldn't go back. She was unwavering in her refusal."

"You should've *made* her go back."

"How? You remember Jane. She trumps us all in stubbornness. If we tried to force her to do something, she'd have ridden away from us as well." Guilt stopped her from being completely honest, from telling Lewis the full truth. As time had passed, she'd learned how to manipulate Jane into doing what she wanted—which was making Jane stay with them.

Gypson finally spoke. "I said Jane could stay with us. It was my decision. Mine alone. If you need to blame someone, that'd be me. Only me."

"All I want is to see Jane." Lewis' words knifed her heart. "Take me to her. Now."

Gaylon shook his head. "We can't. She's gone."

"And we have to find her," Eldora shot back. "When did you last see her?"

"Just before we reached Juniper Flats."

"Then she's nearby! Why didn't you tell me right away?" Still on her knees, she spun toward the door, intent on finding Jane, wherever she was.

Gaylon grabbed her arm. "You wouldn't have listened to anything I said afterward. You would have rushed off half-cocked, like you're about to do now."

"Why did Jane leave you now, after all this time?" Lewis crouched beside her.

"She vowed she'd never return to Juniper Flats."

Lewis' eyes narrowed as if he'd finally caught her in a lie. "She told me she'd come home when she was ready, when she was a star."

"*A star so bright she'd blind you with her brilliance*," Eldora replied. Each word made Lewis stiffen until he was strung tight as a bow. She couldn't look at him. Her gaze skittered to the window, the bed, all around the caravan. How had it miraculously survived a sinking ship unscathed? While Jane hadn't?

"She was with you," Lewis said. "On the steamboat."

She nodded. "When the boat started tipping, the captain was the first to swim for shore."

"Drunk as a skunk," Gaylon muttered, "and kept afloat by a crate of bourbon."

"Almost everyone followed him. Jane and I tried to free as many horses and livestock as we could." The dark despair of that moment threatened to swallow her whole, like the river had. "As the boat rolled over, a wagon pinned Jane to the deck and then took her under."

"I watched you go with her," Gaylon said. "Always inseparable. I knew that if you couldn't free her that day, you'd drown holding onto her. But then you surfaced and Jane lay still as death in your arms."

"Someone dove down and helped us." The selfless act of a stranger lifted her spirits. "I couldn't find him later to thank him."

"And Jane?" Lewis asked.

"Her leg was crushed."

"But she can still ride. Tell me she can. She lives to ride."

"She'll never ride like before. Before the accident, she was..." An image rose in her mind and stole her breath. "She was brilliant. She'd reached for the stars and caught every one. She was a kaleidoscope of light, so bright she held every audience spellbound. She was Eldorado Jane."

"You both were," Gaylon said. "You created that act together and worked every day to make it perfect."

"But she performed while I stayed on the sidelines."

"Until you changed places again." Lewis' words were grim but lacked their previous condemnation.

"We needed the money," Gaylon said. "We'd lost too much in the accident, and we'd signed a contract with Roy. We'd promised to merge our show with his and supply him with the Eldorado Jane act. More importantly, Jane needed expensive treatments to recover as much of her strength as she could."

Lewis closed his eyes, as if rejecting a possibility too horrible to contemplate. "You never answered my question. Can she still ride?"

"I believe so." Her spine straightened with her words. Her belief in Jane had always given her strength. "I believe she can do anything if she puts her whole heart into it. Her body might be banged up, but she's still tougher than anyone I know. But she refuses to try. She hasn't been on a horse since the accident."

"Where would she go?" Lewis asked.

"Somewhere she can remain unseen. Somewhere no one wants to go."

He stared at the ceiling, brow furrowed in thought. "When we were young, our parents told us about a shack on the other side of the highland. A beast without a soul lived there. They said that so we wouldn't go up there exploring. It worked. We never went beyond the headwaters." Lewis met her gaze. "If she hasn't ridden since her accident, she'll be on foot. Could she walk that far with her injury?"

"Her confidence may be lagging, but if she wants to get

somewhere, she will. It'll just take her longer. She uses a leg brace to walk."

"She'll be moving slowly. Limping. Unable to run."

She heard the words he didn't say. *Jane would be the perfect prey for an injured and starving mountain lion.*

"I have to find her." Lewis sprinted out of the caravan.

She chased after him. "I'm going with you."

He careened to a halt at the bottom of the steps. A rising wind caught the dust kicked up from his boots, blew it around them, then away—along with her hopes of riding with him. He was going to tell her to stay behind again.

"Damn," he muttered. "We don't need this now."

The word *we* made her spirits soar. His dire tone brought her back to earth fast.

She scanned the camp, but didn't see any threat. "What's wrong?"

"That." He pointed to the horizon and a dark bank of clouds flashing lightning and rumbling thunder. Driven by the wind, it rolled straight for the highland, and Jane.

POUNDING rain soaked Lewis to the skin, and further, boring into him, pinprick by pinprick—like his conscience. Only a fool rode out in such a storm.

He couldn't see beyond Lila's ears. They wouldn't reach the shack or Jane today. They'd be lucky if they reached the homestead. In this deluge, they could ride past it and never know.

He drew hope from Lila. Head down, sides heaving, she pushed up the hill. Moving faster, like home was one step away. He trusted her instincts more than his own right now.

Despite everything he'd learned in Gypson's caravan, he couldn't stop believing in Eldora.

She followed him on Samson. Once more his shadow. She should've stayed with Gypson. Except that man was a charlatan, the ultimate deceiver. And Eldora still loved him. She'd never stop. Jane probably felt the same way.

Lucky charlatan.

But Eldora had left Gypson and followed him. She wanted to find Jane, but he couldn't help hoping for more. He hadn't had time to ask, and now he couldn't even see her. Not since the rain shrouded everything. She was still with him, though. He felt her presence. He also heard Samson's muffled hoofbeats behind him.

Lila's shoulder jerked down and back. Her hoof screeched, like fingernails on a child's chalkboard. The inevitable impact of her knee hitting the rock jolted deep inside him. So did her fear. Her entire body shuddered as she scrambled to regain her footing, only to slip again and fall on both knees.

His weight kept her down. Sliding backward, then sideways. Gathering speed. Close to rolling. He kicked one foot free of its stirrup and prepared to leap, to take the tumble instead.

Lila slammed to a stop. On the hill below them, Samson stood solid as bedrock with his chest braced against Lila's belly. As they'd slid down the slope, they'd miraculously hit Samson. No. Eldora had maneuvered Samson to stand beneath them and break their fall.

His panic-tight lungs gulped in air. Gypson wasn't the only lucky one.

Eldora yelled something he couldn't hear. The wailing wind whipped it away. She leaned toward him. He did the same.

Finally, her words reached him. "I saw something ahead. It looked..." She shrugged. "Familiar. We're almost there. I know it. But Lila can carry you no further. Get on Samson."

He shook his head. "I won't drag you down with me."

"Samson won't fall. Me, I'm not so certain. My strength is wavering." So was her perch on her saddle. That and the exhaustion etched on her pale face launched him into action.

He took the leap to sit behind her. When he wrapped his arms around her, she leaned into his embrace and stayed there. A perfect fit.

Without his weight pressing her down, Lila clambered up to stand on all four legs. A heartbeat later, she'd surged once again straight up the slope with Samson close behind her—racing toward whatever Eldora had seen ahead.

They rode into a horseshoe of rock holding the cabin and corrals. Home had been only a few strides away.

He helped Eldora down and went to Lila. He ran his hands over her legs, searching for torn flesh and cracked bone. Miraculously, she had none. He removed her saddle and dumped it by the cabin door. Eldora did the same with Samson's.

"The horses." Fear edged her voice higher. The calm confidence she'd used to steady the horses and him during the ride was cracking. "They need shelter."

He pointed to the big corral and yelled, "It's the best we can do." They released their horses there to become one with the herd, hugging the horseshoe wall of rock surrounding the homestead. Eldora's frown reflected the worry in his heart. He should've built a barn when he expanded the corrals, but time had been in short supply.

Buffeted by the wind, Eldora cleaved to his side, adding her strength to his for the return trip to the cabin. At the door, she stayed close as he hoisted a saddle on each hip. Then they went in together. Only their combined efforts shut the door against the gusting wind. The entire cabin rattled and groaned under its continued assault. Inside, their labored breathing eased along with his heartbeat until he heard Eldora's teeth chattering.

They needed to get out of their wet clothes.

One stride took him to the table, where he lit the lantern. "Where's your traveling case? The one you mentioned yesterday."

"Beside the bed, but...I've only a nightgown left."

Her reply thrilled and unnerved him. His heart raced again. How the hell was he going to keep his gaze, and his hands, off her when he saw her wearing only a nightgown in a small room that held...? He inhaled sharply. He'd finally see her in his bed.

Her sigh sounded tired, but also apologetic. "The rest of my clothes, the ones I got muddy yesterday, are hanging outside."

Or they'd blown away in the storm. Either way, they were out of reach. He put the table between them as he went to retrieve her case. When he turned to hand it to her, he bumped into her. She followed him again.

He didn't step away. He couldn't. Not with her sweet body so close, showing him how well they kept fitting together.

His perfect shadow. But also a pale one with wet hair plastered to her head and down the back of his sodden coat. Maybe the dress she wore underneath, the one he'd admired yesterday, wasn't as bad.

"Sorry about your coat." Eyes dark with exhaustion, she blinked up at him.

"It'll be fine once we hang it up to dry."

She slipped free of his coat and handed it to him. His mouth was the first thing to go dry. Her dress hugged her every curve, wet and enticing, begging him to remove it as well, to make her his in every way. But he couldn't. Not completely. She belonged to another man.

If he touched her, he'd be responsible for seducing her into a sin and for the regret she'd surely feel in the morning. She was already frowning as she stared at the ceiling, unable to meet his gaze. She was swaying as well.

He held his coat between them, ready to catch her in it if she fell. "Bet you wish this cabin was bigger. Why don't you sit down?"

She complied and sat on the nearest thing—his bed. She clutched the mattress on either side of her as her gaze went back to the ceiling, and the water he finally noticed dripping down onto the floor.

"My first wish," she said, "is that we're not washed away in a flood."

"You're safe here." Or at least he hoped so. He'd never stood in such an all-consuming storm in his life. He grabbed a bucket to catch the water. Then he hung his coat on the door peg and pressed his brow against the cold, wet cloth. It did little to cool the fever heating his blood.

"You're not thinking about going outside, are you?"

"Nope. I'm thinking you're cold and tired. You need sleep."

"We both do."

"You can use the bed. I'll..." He might just stand here all night.

"I brought your bedroll inside this morning. It's next to the door."

He glanced down. So it was.

"Are you going to turn around?" Her question sounded breathless...almost eager.

More wishful thinking. Dangerous as well.

"Not until you've changed your clothes and crawled under the covers."

Her boots thudded on the floor. Her dress followed with a soggy splat. Sheets rustled. Springs squeaked. Silence followed. Could she have fallen asleep that quickly?

"Aren't you cold? Your clothes look as wet as mine." She wasn't sleeping. She was lying in his bed, wearing only a nightgown and staring at him.

"I've slept in worse," he reminded her while recalling what he'd told her yesterday by the fire pit.

"You're not planning to stay in wet clothes all night?"

"And if I am?"

"It wouldn't be...safe." The last word, the one he'd used so often, held a teasing tone. The next ones came fast and sharp. "You're not catching pneumonia. Not because of me."

"I'll be fine."

The bed squeaked. "I refuse to stay warm in this bed if you won't—"

"Eldora, stop! All I have to wear is what I have on."

"What do you usually sleep in?"

"Nothing."

A long silence followed before she said, "Then do that."

"I can't. It wouldn't be...proper." He didn't care about propriety. He cared how Eldora would feel in the morning if he gave her reason to regret being impulsive with him tonight.

"Good grief," she said. "Stop being a prude. I've seen a naked man before."

That thought did nothing to soothe his frustration. "I'm not your husband."

"When a woman lives and travels with a show whose performers are mostly men, she sees more than her husband, and long before she's married."

Her revelation made his blood pound with jealousy. He ground his teeth to keep quiet.

"I'm not staying snug in your bed if you won't undress, get into your bedroll and get comfortable as well."

He kept grinding his teeth.

"I'm as stubborn as you. I bet I can stay up all night arguing with you. I bet—"

He shoved away from the door with a growl. He kept his back to her as he removed his shirt, boots, and finally his trousers. Behind him, the silence weighed on him. Heavy and unbearable. More discomforting than a ton of wet clothes.

Maybe she didn't like what she saw. Maybe he was no different from any of the men she'd seen before. A fine time to become vain, while standing stark-naked before the only woman whose opinion mattered.

He spread his bedroll on the floor and dove in. He lay on his side, facing the door again, so he wouldn't see the disappointment in her eyes. She probably wasn't even looking. She'd probably rolled over and turned her back to him when he first started disrobing.

"How did you get the scars on your back?"

So, she was looking at him after all. And she'd have to look closely to see those scars, old and faint as they were. The knowledge warmed him and tented his bedroll where his passion rose hottest.

"I took a tumble in a farmer's field, on rocks dug up by his plow." He was lucky he hadn't been rendered blind and deaf that day when the lightning fried a nearby tree and the thunder's shockwave struck him.

"The night you rode in another storm." Her voice had gone soft and soothing again. "With Jane."

Her words cooled him down like nothing else could. Jane was somewhere out there in this storm, and he couldn't reach her. Again.

"How long will it take to ride from here to the shack?" As usual, Eldora had guessed what he was thinking.

"Less than an hour in dry conditions. Twice that slogging through the mud and debris we'll find when this storm blows over."

"I won't stay behind. Not tomorrow. Not ever. No more arguments."

"How about no more secrets either?" he replied.

"Agreed. You should know everything so you can help Jane if...something happens to me and my father."

"Nothing's going to happen to you." When she didn't answer, he rolled over to face her.

She looked even better lying in his bed than she had wearing his coat.

"I'm keeping you safe."

"And my father?" Fear rippled in her voice again.

He struggled for an answer. None of them would resurrect her trust. A lie wouldn't help either.

"No more secrets," she reminded him.

"He's not my main concern."

She shook her head. "Then we are at odds again."

"But your father and I are not. We're both determined to protect you and Jane. That's why you should tell me everything. I asked who your father had killed. You never told me."

She stared at him while the rain beat down on the cabin and his hopes for an answer. Finally, she said, "Do you know anyone from Nebraska?"

# CHAPTER 7

For the second day straight, Lewis tried to focus on a trail winding down from the highland that might conceal a mountain lion. This time he scanned the green juniper and scarlet-berried agarita for a pair of equally dangerous and unpredictable threats: a land-stealing blackmailer and a scarred man from Nebraska.

What he really wanted to see traveled behind him. Eldora riding Samson. Once more his faithful shadow.

All morning she'd stuck close to him as she helped him check the shack. Last night they'd slept only a few feet apart. He hadn't slept much, though. Now the memory of her lying in his bed stifled his yawn better than anything. Eldora, so tantalizingly close, all he had to do was reach out and draw her into his arms.

Her revelation of Gypson and Calhoun's past in Nebraska had distracted him, along with something else. She may have shared her secrets, but she could no longer trust him. How could she? He didn't even trust himself. Not after the way he'd threatened Gypson.

His hatred for Gaylon Gypson had consumed him.

One thing had stopped him from acting on his rage. Gypson truly loved Eldora and Jane. In a world with growing threats, he'd be a fool to reject an ally whose primary goal matched his: keep both Eldora and Jane safe.

He needed more allies if he was going to succeed. That mission, plus one more, had him on this trail today. Eldora had also helped him complete Sadie's request to check the headwaters. They flowed as before, except for the creeks leading to one place. The Ballantyne Ranch.

"Can we go back tomorrow?" Behind him, Eldora still sounded sleepy from their early morning start. Her voice also sounded sweet and thick, like honey straight from the hive.

"We shouldn't. Not too often." Someone had been in the shack beyond the headwaters. They just couldn't tell who. "If it's Jane up there, she needs to feel safe enough to stay put and rest." He refrained from saying Eldora needed to find a place where she could do the same.

"Jane won't leave," she said, "if it's only the two of us coming to see her."

Maybe she'd stay for Eldora. He doubted she'd stay for him. Jane's vow to never return hounded him like a black cloud on the horizon. "We left enough food to last several days." They'd also left a warning note about the mountain lion tacked to the door. "We'll head up with more when it's needed. Maybe we'll see her then."

"And today? Why aren't we returning to the cabin?"

"What makes you think we aren't?"

"The trees are...changing while the slope levels out and the air loses its crispness. We're leaving the highland, so the homestead must be behind us."

Her observation reminded him of what she'd said in the storm, before they reached the homestead. She'd seen something familiar. She was learning to read the land, losing the anxiety it previously inspired. But what she'd learned today made her sound more irritated that relaxed. Like the only place she wanted to go was the homestead.

Or was that just wishful thinking?

"Nothing is familiar about this trail," she added. "So I'm guessing we aren't heading to town. I've never seen so many of these glossy-green trees."

"They're called cedar elm. Their spring leaves glisten next to their duller neighbors. On the trail from town to the homestead, you'll see this thicket in the distance. It's where you'd turn if you wanted to visit the Ballantynes."

He reined Lila around a tree felled by the storm. The opportunity to sneak a glance at Eldora was lost in the task of finding a safe path through thick mud around roots ripped from the earth and thrust into the air like talons.

"Are we headed there now?" she asked.

"We are."

"Really?" For the first time since finding the shack and not finding Jane, excitement rose in her voice. "I always wanted to see the Ballantyne Ranch. Your family's as well."

Her delight made him laugh. His concerns retreated when she joined him, but only for an instant. "Today we've time for one visit. Maybe I can take you to my family's ranch tomorrow."

"Tomorrow, I'm..." Her voice faded away with uncertainty. When she spoke again, her words were brisk. "I'm going to see my father."

"Why?" He stiffened, wishing he could take back the question. Gypson's cough had sounded deep and dire. An illness like that usually heralded the end of a man.

"I'm going for the same reason you're visiting the Ballantynes. You count them as family even though...they're not."

Contemplating Gypson's revelation that she wasn't his birth daughter made her sound lonely. Deeply lonely. Like the feeling was a familiar companion.

That couldn't be possible. She was the star of a big show, surrounded every day by adoring admirers. That's what she missed.

He strove for a topic to distract her, and him, from her impending departure from his life. "Families form in unexpected ways. Noah and I counted the Doritys in ours. In certain ways, they raised me along with Noah and Jacob."

Eldora inhaled a long breath as if she'd finally solved a puzzle she'd been brooding over. "You're hoping Noah might know why a blackmailer or the scarred man from Nebraska would want the Dority land. That's why you're taking me to his ranch."

"And I want you to finally meet him and Sadie." He strove to keep his tone light. "I want you to feel comfortable going to them if you need anything."

"What might I need?" Her question was sharp with suspicion.

*Someone to help you if your father and I can't.* Another topic he'd regret if embarked upon. He searched for an alternative. "How about advice from a woman who's seen her share of challenges? Sadie's good at making the most of difficult situations."

"I thought Noah's wife was happy out here."

"She is, but she wasn't in Dodge City or any of the places she lived before. That's her story to tell, though. Not mine."

Her sigh joined the breeze rustling the leaves. "Remind me again what you're trying to tell me."

"Remember this trail, so you can go to the Ballantyne Ranch instead of town if you...get bored of my company."

The creak of saddle leather and squelch of hooves slogging through more mud grew unduly loud as he waited for her reply.

Finally, she said, "You think they'll welcome a stranger? One who came to steal your land?"

"You came for Jane," he reminded her.

She inhaled sharply. "Of course! Noah and Jane knew each other. She might go to him or feel safe hiding on his land. We need to tell the Ballantynes to watch for her."

He stifled his groan. Eldora trusted everyone to help Jane, but she still couldn't believe they'd help her. Only time would prove her wrong. Time was running out, though, if she planned to return to town. With her father's failing health, she wouldn't come back. Family trumped every card. All bets were off.

The trees gave way to prairie with clumps of elbow bush. Their tiny yellow-green flowers contrasted with Samson's ebony body as Eldora urged him forward to trot beside Lila.

Once again, her hair was restrained in a tight braid secured with the ribbon he'd returned this morning. The taming of her hair only emphasized the spark in her eyes. In equal measure, she both entranced and unnerved him. His daredevil angel was planning something.

"The sooner we get to their ranch," she said, "the sooner we can talk to them. Let's race!"

He caught Samson's rein, prepared to tell her to slow down, that she couldn't race and memorize the trail. The disappearance of her smile stopped him.

He let go. He let the pure bliss of racing beside Eldora push everything else aside. Her laughter was the potion that made everything possible.

Too soon, the Ballantyne Ranch appeared ahead, and their race ended. Clusters of longhorn cattle dotted the land, as did the stragglers being rounded up by men on horseback. Only yesterday's rain prevented them from raising a cloud of dust. One day of rain had helped, but it wouldn't save the Ballantyne Ranch.

When he slowed Lila to a trot, Eldora did the same with Samson. He scanned the cowhands, searching for a dappled gray mount with a rider who'd sit taller than the others. He found his quarry already loping toward him.

He urged Lila forward to meet him. "Why the roundup?"

Noah tipped his hat to Eldora before answering him. "We're putting together another drive to Dodge."

He felt his jaw drop. "You said you'd never go there again."

"And I'm not. Got an offer to add my herd to a neighbor's going north." Noah's gaze returned to Eldora. "You must be Mrs. Calhoun. Glad Lewis finally brought you for a visit. Wish he remembered his manners, though." He reached across the space separating them. "I'm Noah."

She shook his hand eagerly, but her voice was stilted when she said, "My name is actually Eldora Gypson."

Noah held on to her hand. "And are you Jane Dority as well?"

Eldora met his gaze without blinking. "No. I'm not."

"Thank you for your honesty. Sometimes a lie is necessary, but the truth frees the soul." A smile tugged Noah's lips as he released her hand. "Truth is, you remind me of Jane."

Eldora's nod lacked enthusiasm. "We share the same plain looks."

She and Jane were anything but plain. Before he could say so, Noah spoke.

"The resemblance is primarily in your riding. Lewis said your talent on a horse reminded him of Jane. I'm inclined to agree. So what's brought you racing to my home today?"

Lewis needed to focus on Jane and Eldora, but a brand

new worry wouldn't let him. "Who's volunteered to lead the drive?"

Noah snorted in disbelief. "You need to ask?"

"She can't go." The knot in his gut tightened. "It's too dangerous

"You gonna be the one to convince Lee of that?"

"Lee?" Eldora sounded more intrigued than surprised. "As in your sister, Oralee?"

"His sister looked after our ranches while we drove our herds to Dodge," Noah replied, using the tone he always used when talking about either of Lewis' sisters. It left no doubt he'd be proud to call them his sisters as well. "She's the reason I had a home to return to, and that Lewis earned enough to stop chasing cattle and hang out with his horses."

"Olivia helped as well."

"True. But her heart isn't set on learning every detail about the cattle business. She's got other plans."

"I don't like either of their plans. Running a ranch is a helluva lot different than months enduring the worst trail conditions before reaching that cesspit of sin called Dodge." He shook his head. Oralee wasn't going there. "The Adams Ranch has no pressing need to partake in a cattle drive. My sisters never mentioned water troubles."

Noah stared at his cattle, his men, his land—avoiding Lewis and Eldora. "Maybe they didn't want to add to your load when you rode in with warnings of prickly wild cats and other challenges."

"You mean me," Eldora replied without hesitation. "I'm not here for the water, and the creeks feeding the Adams Ranch are fine. We checked."

Noah went very still. "Why'd you do that?"

"Someone asked me to," Lewis snapped. "Do you need to ask who?"

Noah's gaze went straight to the ranch house.

"Your wife was wise to be concerned," Eldora said in a softer tone than he'd used. "Only your creeks have been tampered with."

"So," Noah drawled, "the ladies are looking out for us again. Someone's stolen our water and wants to steal your land." He contemplated Eldora. "Why do you want the Dority homestead?"

"The only thing I want is to keep Jane away from the blackmailer who wants the land."

"We don't know his identity," Lewis said.

"Or why he wants the land," Eldora added.

"Pretty hard to get anywhere knowing neither." Noah held up his hand to stop further comment. "Let's discuss the rest with Sadie. I'll meet you at the house after I tell the men to carry on without me." Noah reined his gray around and galloped off.

Eldora shaded her eyes with one hand as she stared at the ranch house in the distance. "Is that Noah's wife on the porch?"

A flash of red hair told him it was. "Sadie's waiting for us." He waited as well—for Eldora to propose a race to the house.

She didn't. She sat still as a statue on Samson. Only her gaze moved, darting away from the house like she wanted to flee into the hills.

# CHAPTER 8

*F*or an unbearable moment, meeting Noah and admitting she'd impersonated his friend had filled Eldora with a crippling self-doubt. But Noah was right. The truth had set her free. So had his firm handshake and gracious acceptance of her deceit and candor.

Noah and Lewis not only lived up to Jane's stories, they exceeded them.

Jane had no stories about Sadie. She'd never met Noah's wife. Other than the handful of comments Lewis had made, Sadie was a complete unknown. Why did it make a difference? She didn't know, but it did.

The prospect of meeting Sadie made her want to run the other way.

When she reached the Ballantyne's house, vanity joined the emotions playing havoc with her fortitude. Whatever Lewis had seen in her to invoke the label of daredevil was long gone. She'd never felt more lackluster standing next to Sadie, with her vibrant red hair and green eyes.

Sadie's freckles might not be deemed stylish by New Yorkers, or any who coveted porcelain complexions, but out here Sadie's appeal was undeniable, as was her strength and affection.

Despite holding a squirming one-year-old on her hip, she managed to embrace Lewis in a warm welcome. A familiar one. Lewis was blessed to count the Ballantynes as friends. More than friends. Family.

Mastering a new riding routine suddenly seemed easy compared to turning a stranger into a friend. She held out her hand and prayed it was steady.

Sadie ignored her handshake and hugged her as well. Sadie's unhesitating acceptance astounded her. When Sadie released her, her son did not. He clutched Eldora's braid in his tiny fist.

"I see Jacob's happy to meet you as well." Sadie smiled at her son. "Do you like the lady's hair?"

Jacob nodded. "Pretty lady."

His declaration left her bewildered and floundering for a reply.

"I agree," Lewis said. "And I'm not surprised those are some of his first words, considering how many times he's heard them in this house."

Jacob had his mother's eyes and his father's darker auburn hair. She'd never thought much about having children and hadn't been disappointed when her union with Roy failed to produce any. Now staring at Jacob, she yearned to hold a child with Lewis' wild blond hair and hazel eyes.

"Do you want to hold Jacob?"

The instant Sadie asked, Jacob released her braid and eagerly held out his hands.

Eldora stepped out of reach. If she held him, she might never want to let go. "I wouldn't want to...drop him."

"That'd never happen." Lewis stepped forward, and Jacob leapt into his arms. "This little feller's got a powerful grip. I could doze off standing up and he'd still be hanging on to me come morning."

"You look tired," Sadie said. "You both do."

Sheer exhaustion had made her fall asleep last night and robbed her of the chance of making the most of sharing a night with Lewis. What she'd seen before he'd dove into his bedroll had supplied her with wonderful memories, though.

Lewis studied her face. "We could've delayed our visit. I should've taken you straight home so you could sleep."

"When did your show arrive?" Sadie asked.

Eldora blinked in surprise. "How did you know?"

"Lewis just said so." A frown creased Sadie's brow. "He mentioned your home. Last time he visited, he said your home was a traveling show. I assumed it'd be following you and would arrive sooner or later. You must be relieved to be reunited with it."

Suddenly, standing on the porch felt very hot. "I'm still staying at the Dority homestead."

"But your troupe is in Juniper Flats?"

She nodded.

Sadie smiled. "Small spaces bring us together. I only began to appreciate my tiny room in Dodge once Noah was in it." Sadie ran a loving hand over Jacob's hair, then gestured for them to follow her inside the house. "Come in and rest for a while."

Sadie's easy manner made her follow without hesitation. So did an intense curiosity to know what had happened in Dodge. The room they entered was anything but small, with a mammoth fireplace made of field stones, a gleaming cast-iron stove, and a table whose length could've easily accommodated more than the current ten chairs.

Sadie gestured to the table. "Have a seat. I'll bring coffee and food."

Jacob now had a firm grip on Lewis' hat. When Lewis transferred it from his head to Jacob's, the boy's higher pitched giggles and Lewis' deeper laughter created a magical tune that held her spellbound.

Lewis' laughter faded, but his grin grew when he caught her watching them. "Sure you don't want to hold him?"

She shook her head. She wasn't sure about anything anymore.

Boots, with jingling spurs, bounded up the porch steps. Noah made a beeline for his wife and kissed her nose. "I think I see a new freckle. Have you been flirting with the sun again, pretty lady?"

"What if I have?" Sadie ran her hand over her husband's hair in the same loving manner she'd used on her son. "My garden needed tending after the storm."

"This new freckle needs attention as well." Noah pressed his lips to her cheekbone.

"Ha. You missed. It's over here." Sadie pointed to her other cheek, and Noah took his time kissing his way to that location.

Lewis claimed a seat at the table and occupied himself by tickling Jacob. An overpowering urge made Eldora want to kiss him with the same love Noah and Sadie exhibited. Lewis' gaze met hers, and everything went quiet. Like the heady moment before a show started when everyone held their breath with anticipation.

She lived for those moments. None had ever been this intoxicating.

Someone cleared their throat. Lewis' gaze jumped to his friends who now sat at the table, staring at them expectantly. When Eldora realized she was the only one standing, she slid onto the nearest chair.

"Did you say something?" Lewis' drawl sounded deeper than usual.

Noah nodded. "Said grub and coffee are on the table if you're interested."

"Thank you." Lewis bounced Jacob on his knee, entertaining the boy and also distracting him from grabbing the hot coffee pot as he poured a cup for her and him.

The sight warmed her as much as the coffee did.

Noah put his arm around his wife's shoulders. "I was also bringing Sadie up to speed about the stranger wanting your land. What do you know about him?"

Eldora spoke rapidly, eager to pursue that subject and not her chaotic feelings for Lewis. "Just that he sent letters demanding Roy Calhoun gain control of the land via me. He believes I have a claim to the land, that I'm Jane Dority and that I'm still Roy's wife. But none of that is true."

Lewis set down his cup with a jarring clunk. He stared at her with wide eyes that suddenly narrowed into a look of hunger. "You're not married?"

After wanting to tell him for so long, part of her now wished she hadn't. She felt exposed, stripped of an armor that had previously protected her. What if she'd misjudged Lewis' reactions? What if her overwhelming attraction for him had made her believe he felt the same for her? What if he rejected her now?

She couldn't hide from the possibility. "I obtained a divorce a few weeks ago. I couldn't tell anyone because my plan hinged on being Jane and married to Roy."

"You couldn't tell me..." Lewis' gaze dropped to the coffee cup still clutched in his hand. "Last night?"

"I thought only Roy held the power to hoodwink me.

Turned out I didn't know my father very well either. Maybe I only see what I want to see in others. I don't trust myself anymore."

"You should," Sadie said. "Trust frees the soul."

Eldora glanced at Noah. "Didn't you say the truth did that?"

"Trust and the truth go hand in hand." He laid his hand, palm up, on the table.

Sadie immediately put her hand in his. "I know escaping a life of lies isn't easy. I also know it's better not done alone."

Eldora told them everything she knew, ending with the shack on the other side of the highland. "Someone had been there, but we couldn't tell if it was Jane. We thought she might come here instead."

"Do you have a picture of her?" Sadie asked.

"Jane was never keen to pose for them. After the accident, she flat-out refused. Look for someone like me. My hair, my size and looks."

"Different eyes." Lewis finally released his cup and pulled a crumpled paper from his pocket. He smoothed the water damaged sheet flat on the table. "Watch out for Colonel Calhoun as well." He tapped his finger on Roy's face.

Sadie gasped and drew the picture closer. "I've seen him before."

"He came to your ranch?" Lewis asked.

"Why didn't you tell me?" Noah's jaw tightened with worry. "You know you can tell me anything, right?"

"I know that now." Sadie released the show poster and set her hand gently against her husband's face, which immediately relaxed. "But I saw this man long ago—in Dodge after your cattle destroyed my farm and before you came back for me."

"Your show performed in Dodge?" Lewis asked Eldora. She shook her head.

So did Sadie. "Calhoun was alone, or at least he was when I saw him. Edward and I came out of our room at the Great Western as he went into Robert Wardell's."

"Wardell," Noah said the name like a curse.

"I've never met anyone by that name or heard anyone mention him," Eldora said. "Who is he?"

Sadie grimaced. "A conniving cattle buyer who wanted to control Dodge City and everyone in it, including me. He reveled in the exploitation of other's misfortune."

"Control." Saying the word made Eldora grimace as well. "Someone's altering the highland creeks to deprive you of water and destroy your livelihood. Can we stop them?"

"The owner of the Dority land could," Lewis replied in a dour tone. "The homestead is small, but its land stretches like a band between the headwaters and the Ballantyne Ranch...and my family's land, our neighbors, and Juniper Flats as well."

"Control the Dority land and you control the water supply." That was the answer she'd been searching for ever since she'd come to the homestead. "That's why the blackmailer wants the land. Could he be Wardell?"

"Could be a lot of people." Noah stared at a tintype on the mantel behind him. The image held a tall man with his arm around a woman who smiled up at him in adoration. "Out here, water drowns men in greed. It started the range dispute that led to my father's death and my mother's as well."

She couldn't stand the thought of Sadie and Noah suffering a similar fate.

"My mother couldn't live without my father," Noah added.

Eldora was starting to feel the same way about Lewis.

Lewis stared at the ceiling and spoke with quiet deliberation. "If Wardell is the blackmailer...then Calhoun's up against a master manipulator holding an ace card—Calhoun's past in Nebraska. He'd do whatever Wardell demands. They've started with theft and altering waterways. What if their next move is murder?"

Eldora flinched. She couldn't let that outcome happen. She pressed her palm against her heart in an attempt to slow its hammering pace. She needed to calm down so she could think.

If Roy knew Wardell, then her father might as well. She must return to the show and find out. The same thought, along with an avalanche of worry, was reflected in Lewis' frown as he stared at her. He was pondering ways to make her stay at the cabin while he went to town without her.

She knew because she was thinking the same thing.

The first step was getting Lewis back to the homestead. Then she'd tell him she didn't trust him, so they must part ways. The hungry intensity that had narrowed his eyes when he'd first heard she wasn't married had returned. She'd have to tell him something bigger.

Whatever she said, it probably wouldn't stop Lewis from following her to town.

She'd have to sneak away in the night. That was the only way she'd buy Lewis a few hours of safety while she questioned her father and then confronted Roy.

As soon as she confirmed the blackmailer's identity, she must ride as fast as she could to the nearest lawman. She prayed he wasn't being controlled as well and that she had the strength and luck to reach him before anything happened to Lewis or her new friends.

"Do you smell that?" Eldora lifted her nose and her gaze. A lazy plume of soft gray drifted over a familiar tree line. "Smoke." She glanced at Lewis riding beside her. "It's coming from the homestead, isn't it?"

Lewis didn't meet her gaze. He continued frowning at the smoke. Then, like a spring bubbling from the earth, his brow rose with wonder. "It's coming from the fire pit by the cabin."

She scanned the smoke again, wanting to share his excitement. Only a tight knot of anxiety grew inside her. She felt...territorial. "Someone's made themselves at home."

"Jane." The single word and Lewis' smile blew all of her irritation away.

"Let's race home and see her!"

His smile faded. "Lead the way. I'll be right behind you."

The knot inside her returned. "What's wrong?"

"Jane might not recognize me. I won't chance spooking her and making her run away from me again." His gaze scanned the trees ahead with longing, but he reined Lila to a stop. "I won't spoil this one chance."

She sealed her lips against telling him he was wrong. Better to show him that Jane would meet him with open arms. And while they were having their reunion, she could sneak back to the show and keep them both safe.

She urged Samson forward.

He went willingly. He knew the way home.

*Home.*

The word echoed in her blood, strong and true. Jane had come home. Lila's hoofbeats came close behind her. A sound sweeter even than the crisp scent of pine filling her lungs while sunbeams streamed through branches sighing in the wind: *Home. Home. We're all home.*

How had Jane ever left this place? It wasn't only nature that was cruel, but life itself. Now that she must leave, her entire being—body, heart, and soul—wanted to stay. The memory of Lewis' words joined the wind, *Stay with me, Angel Eyes.*

Maybe she could. Maybe with Jane's return, she could find a way. A cocoon of hope and rightness enveloped her as Samson broke through the trees and she saw the Dority homestead. Her euphoria faded to disappointment, then spiked into alarm, sharp enough to steal her breath.

Samson slammed to a halt, tense and quivering beneath her. Her fear had become his.

Two men, as different as night and day, sat on opposite sides of the fire pit. As far from each other as the circle of stone would allow. Looking as tense as she felt, the men possessed one similarity—hands reaching for their favorite weapons, an unadorned tomahawk and a sleek Winchester '76 repeating rifle.

Had Roy sent one of them, or even both, to kill Lewis?

Lewis and Lila skidded to a stop between her and the men. He glared down the barrel of his old Henry rifle at them.

Vandrill and Hawk carefully raised their hands. No one moved in the brittle silence that followed. The men's mounts stood behind them, tethered outside the small corral. Saddled and waiting to return to the show. She struggled for something to say to make them leave.

Before she could, Hawk spoke in a tone as somber as a graveyard. "You've every right to shoot us."

Vandrill shot him a glare. "You're not helping matters.

You hardly ever do." His gaze snapped back to her. "The colonel sent us to escort you back to town."

She stifled the urge to tell them she was never going back to Roy. She focused on bottling up her emotions, on keeping her face and her voice neutral. "What's in town to warrant this sudden change?"

Hawk and Vandrill exchanged a hasty glance but said nothing.

Their odd behavior shattered her quest for calm faster than any words could. "And since when do I need an escort?" When no one answered, her temper flared red hot. "Tell me!"

"Better if the colonel tells you," Vandrill replied.

"Better for whom?" Lewis asked. "You both heard Calhoun tell her to stay here."

Vandrill shook his head. "Things have changed."

"Yes. They have." She stared at the horses in Lewis' corral, searching for a calming sanctuary there. She didn't find it. "I have a job to do here." She wasn't going with them. She was leaving on her own, in the night, so Lewis couldn't follow.

"Your job is in town. The show is waiting for you there." Vandrill's voice grew stronger, more certain. "I'm sure that will change your mind."

"You know nothing about me and, truth be told, I know nothing about you. I'd be a fool to go anywhere with you."

Vandrill's voice went uncharacteristically soft. "I know you don't trust me. I can't change that. But you can trust Hawk."

"I don't trust either of you. I want you both to leave!"

Neither man moved.

"The lady asked you to leave, as nicely as she could,"

Lewis drawled. "I won't even ask. I'd rather empty this rifle in you."

Vandrill ignored him and kept his gaze on her. "We can't leave without you. You must rejoin the show. It needs you."

Strangely, she no longer needed it. All she needed was Lewis and Jane. She shook her head. "The show can wait."

"But your father cannot." The hushed words came from Hawk.

Fear rumbled in her veins like thunder heralding a storm. She'd forgotten about her father.

Hawk's gaze finally met hers, dark and stormy, her pain reflected there. "I'm sorry I didn't keep watch more closely. We found him, this morning, on the trail heading here. He had many wounds from...what looked like the claws of a large cat."

"The mountain lion." A tawny blur filled her vision. A flash of claws and teeth. *Sharp. Merciless. Unstoppable.*

Something big and gentle settled on her hand. She glanced down to find Lewis' hand holding hers, his rifle back in its scabbard.

"Juniper Flats doesn't have a doctor." His voice sounded far away. "Does your show have one?"

She shook her head while a gray tunnel narrowed her vision.

Lewis' hand tightened around hers, and his ragged whisper brushed her ear. "We'll go to him immediately." He lifted his head, and his words rang loud and clear. "Where is her father?"

"He—" Hawk stood abruptly and kicked dirt over the fire. The remains of her hope blew away with the last puff of smoke. Hawk hadn't used his hand signals. No reassurances. No hiding from the truth. Nobody was safe. "Gaylon lies in his caravan, waiting for his family to attend his burial."

# CHAPTER 9

*Gaylon. Father.* Until she'd traveled to the Dority homestead, Eldora couldn't remember a day without him. He couldn't be dead.

She'd misheard Hawk's words. If she'd waited, she would've seen his hand signals: *All safe.* Instead, she'd urged Samson down the hill and hadn't stopped. A branch slapped her face as they barreled toward town like a locomotive at full steam. The tears stinging her eyes spilled onto her cheeks.

"Slow down!" The shout echoed off the trees, seeming to come from every direction.

Somewhere behind her rode Vandrill and Hawk, and probably Lewis as well. She hadn't looked back to check. The trees swept by in a blur. She didn't care if anything lurked in them. No one would stop her at this speed.

She gritted her teeth and held on to Samson. Words no longer mattered. She'd learn what she needed at the caravan. Gaylon would amble out to meet her or greet her inside with his shotgun. He hadn't survived this long without being smart and stubborn. *Tenacious.* But he was ill. That damned cough. She should never have left him. She should've stayed and protected him.

But the blackmailer demanded she steal the Dority's land. Then Jane had left the show. Maybe she'd gone back. Maybe Jane was waiting at the caravan. Everything would be all right as soon as she got there.

Trees turned into fields and a town of plain but sturdy clapboard buildings and open-faced people who couldn't help but stop and stare with concern and curiosity. Her whole life was a show. Always had been.

She hid her face against Samson's neck and put her trust in him. He knew the way. She didn't want to look at the show camp either. If she did, she'd know the truth she'd tried to ignore all the way down the hill.

*Everything had changed.*

The buzz of unsettled voices ahead confirmed it. She couldn't hide any longer. She lifted her head. A knot of performers circled the tail end of Gaylon's caravan. Roy stood on the steps to the door—standing between her and her father.

When his perturbed gaze jumped from the crowd to her, an unfamiliar expression pinched his face. Uncertainty? Guilt? Fear? Whatever it was, it fled as fast as it came, replaced by his usual cocky expression. He crossed his arms and leaned against the caravan's door.

She jumped off Samson and pushed through the throng. They stepped aside, whispering more words she chose to ignore, until only Roy remained between her and her father.

"Get out of my way." Her voice was shrill in her ears. "You can't stop me from seeing him."

"I do not intend to. But your father no longer resides here. A cowardly sheriff took his body when I wasn't looking and locked him in the town jail."

Grief slammed her to a halt and left her gasping for air. *Your father's body.* The crowd pressed closer, offering their condolences. She could no longer block out the words and hide from the truth. Gaylon was gone. Not even his body remained.

She lifted her chin. "Why would anyone take his body?"

"Because this town is run by an opportunistic civil servant eager to benefit from our misfortune. He no doubt seeks to slander our show's good name. We shall have to pay him to speak the truth."

"We'd chip in our share," someone in the crowd yelled. "If we got paid!"

"What happened to the payroll?" Eldora scanned their frustrated faces.

"Hell if we know. We haven't been paid in weeks, and he won't tell us why."

Roy's brow puckered with exaggerated sadness. "I wished to spare my wife, but I see it can no longer be avoided. Her father took the payroll to keep a blackmailer silent about his wrongdoings in this very town."

"Gaylon isn't a thief!" Her throat closed up. Gaylon was gone. But his memory wasn't. He hadn't stolen Jane or her, and he'd never stolen money. She'd make sure those truths were known. "He wasn't like you. All you care about is wealth and prestige. Gaylon cherished his family and friends. I should never have left him. I'm going to him now." She turned toward town. She'd ask for directions to the jail there.

"You cannot help him." Roy's voice boomed above the muttering of the crowd. "But you can help those friends you mentioned. Gaylon endangered us all by bringing our troupe here. He disobeyed my orders."

"He had to!" The shout came from the crowd, followed by more.

"No one knew when you was comin' back."

"Only way to get money to eat was to move to another town."

"Gaylon agreed. He didn't want us to starve."

The crowd hurled a flurry of complaints and curses at Roy. The decency of a quiet burial surrounded by friends was not in the cards. Her father's life and death had become an opportunity to be used by everyone.

"You all contributed to his death," Roy shouted overtop of them again. "He would be alive if everyone had obeyed my orders."

Shock ripped through her. "What are you saying?" *And what aren't you saying?* "His death wasn't a mountain lion attack?"

"Of course, it was."

She surged toward him. "Tell me the truth!"

When she reached the base of the steps, Roy leaned down and seized her arm. He shook her hard enough to rattle her teeth. "The truth is you know your father would not have been anywhere near the threats circling us if you had both done as you were told."

Roy released her with a howl. Lewis stood beside her, grasping Roy's wrist.

"Keep your hands off the lady." He shoved Roy away.

Roy massaged his arm and glared at Lewis. "*The lady* has been my wife for ten years. I know her. You do not. She is distraught, overcome by the hysteria that is common to her gender. She was this way when I first met her."

"You took advantage of her grief when that boat sank."

Roy's glare grew thunderous. "I protected her from herself. I will do the same today. The sheriff will use her weakness to spread more lies and demand more money. He is nothing more than a greedy opportunist seeking to benefit from our misfortune. You are no different."

"That's a lie," Eldora yelled. "Lewis has done nothing but help me. If you say otherwise, then you're probably lying about everything."

"Control your tongue and your emotions. This man is an outsider. He is not welcome here. He will return to his meager little dirt patch in the hills, and you will stay here with me. Only I know what is best for you."

"She doesn't belong to you anymore." Lewis' words sliced the air like the crack of a whip.

Roy's eyes flickered with surprise and then narrowed. He'd guessed she'd told Lewis about their divorce. "Are you saying my *wife* is now your adulterous *whore*?"

Lewis' hand shot out again. He yanked Roy off his feet and the stairs. Fringed jacket flapping, Roy hit the ground with a wallop and a roar.

Lewis crouched by Roy's side and seized his shirtfront. "I'm saying…" He drew back his fist. "You're an egotistical, foul-mouthed, lying sonuva—"

A man with white-blond hair and a dark-blue jacket swept by her. Vandrill grabbed Lewis from behind and yanked him off Roy. Then he kept him off by locking an arm around his neck.

"Why do you protect this despicable wretch?" Lewis snarled. "Release me."

"Not until everyone calms down," Vandrill replied mildly. "None of us have time for brawling or visiting the sheriff"—his gaze lingered on her before sweeping the crowd—"or arguing about the past. The show starts in thirty minutes."

Tears of disbelief stung her eyes as she glared at Roy. "You booked a performance on the day my father died?"

Roy lurched to his feet and jerked his jacket straight. "Sentimentality is a luxury we cannot afford. Not if we want to pay the vultures circling. If we do not work together, each of us will lose what we hold dear. Everyone must do their job."

"What if the sheriff comes back?" The crowd was rumbling again. "What do we say?"

"Tell him Mr. Adams threatened me with bodily harm. Perhaps the lawman will finally be of service and take this troublemaker to his jail as well."

"My father wasn't the enemy, and neither is Lewis."

Roy folded his arms. "You are either with us or against us." He raised one brow in challenge. "Will you abandon your friends and what is left of your family when they need you most? Will you reject the protection only a husband can provide?"

He was reminding her that if she didn't keep to their agreement and pretense of marriage, the blackmailer might look for another way to get the Dority land. And the only other way was Jane.

Roy's arrogant smile returned as he read her answer on her face.

"You don't have to do this," Lewis said. "We'll find another way."

Roy gestured for her to hurry up. "Say the words, Eldora. Whose side are you on?"

"Yours."

"And you're still my wife?"

She raised her chin. "I'm your prized act."

Roy laughed. "Yes, you are. Only Eldorado Jane can pack the big tent with enough patrons to buy a burial for a man with as many sins as Gaylon Gypson. You are not going anywhere."

"Just like Gaylon," she replied.

Roy's grin slipped. "What?"

"Standing by your side is a family cross to bear." She turned to Lewis. "Whatever happens next, I'm glad I got to meet you. Please look after our friend."

"I can't let you do this." He reached for her, and she did the same.

She flung her arms around his neck and held him tight. The rock-solid strength of his body and the tenderness of his embrace soothed and strengthened her more than anything or anyone she'd ever known. Jane needed this. Jane needed him.

"You cannot protect us both." She whispered the words close to his ear, so only he would hear. "Go find her." She tried to pull away, but he held her tight.

A shudder shook him, and then...he opened his arms. She ducked her head so she wouldn't see his face and change her mind. She unbuckled the gun belt he'd given her and handed it back to him. "Stay safe," she whispered and then fled toward the big tent.

Only Roy's heavy footsteps followed her.

She didn't look at him as she said, "Gaylon gets a proper burial."

He slowed to a stroll, forcing her to match his pace. "Maybe he does, and maybe he does not. You do not give the orders, Little Miss Hoity-Toity."

The name curled around her like a tendril of smoke, then drifted away. It didn't hurt her as it had before. All she felt was numb. "Today I do. Gaylon told me he was the nameless soldier who stood by your side during the glorious Nebraska battle that launched your career. Only he didn't do it for the glory. He never did. He deserves to finally rest in peace."

"How much did he tell you?" Roy's question held an unnatural quietness.

"Everything. But I won't repeat it. I want a quiet burial for my father."

"That is up to the sheriff." Roy's voice was back to being cocky.

"And all he wants is money, right? Did he come up with the idea, or did you?"

"What idea?"

She stopped walking so she could look him fully in the face. "The idea to hold Gaylon's body for ransom. The sheriff is controlling you, or you're controlling him. Either way, you're giving him money."

"And you are wading into dangerous waters," Roy growled.

"That's the thing about being a prized act. If you hurt me, I cannot perform and make money to help save your show."

He stepped forward, so they stood toe-to-toe and loomed over her. "Think about Dory. She's the only family you have left."

Jane had been smart to leave. Was Roy saying he knew where she'd gone? Even if he didn't, he might know soon. He might also realize that Eldora had lied to him, that Dory was really Jane.

Eldora made herself stand firm. "I've never stopped thinking of Dory. Hurt her and I'm gone."

He spat out an incredulous laugh. "Where will you go?"

"To hell, of course." She leaned closer to him. "But don't worry. I won't leave your side. You'll be coming with me."

As the sun descended and dyed the horizon red, Lewis stood in the growing gloom, watching the cast of *Colonel Calhoun's Wondrous West* scurry around a hastily erected staging area behind the big tent. Eldora wasn't the only one missing Gaylon Gypson and whatever the old man had done to help mold these chaotic personalities into the country's finest Wild West extravaganza.

At the head of a colorful string of characters jostling each other to pull props and costumes from a jumble of wooden crates, Eldora sat sidesaddle on Samson with regal stillness. The star of the show, she shone like a beacon in pearly white satin and sparkling rhinestones. Below her snug-as-a-corset jacket, a mid-thigh skirt billowed over wide-legged trousers with a Spanish flair.

Only her hands, covered in ivory leather, moved, stroking Samson's ebony neck. Her face was set, emotionless. She stared straight ahead, waiting for her cue.

Inside the tent, his neighbors—from town and country —buzzed with anticipation and no small amount of incredulity. A show that usually entertained New York's finest had for unknown reasons chosen to visit their small community.

Cradling his Winchester in the crook of his arm, Vandrill stepped out of the shadows to stand beside him.

Lewis' hand itched, wanting to hold the revolver Eldora had returned to him. Instead, he left the handgun in the holster on his hip and focused on Vandrill. The man scanned not the performers or the tent with its audience, but the town on the other side of the field.

"Looking for anything in particular?" Lewis asked.

"You'd best watch your back. Or even better, get your sorry backside far away from here."

Lewis suddenly wished he'd kept his Henry rifle with him, instead of stowing it with Lila in the town's livery. "Any particular threat I should be worried about?"

Vandrill snorted. "Besides the colonel being cross about you and his wife?"

"She's not—" He stopped short of saying Eldora was no longer Calhoun's wife. That was her secret to tell, not his. "She's a lady."

"Yes, she is, but the colonel is no gentleman. Neither is your town's sheriff."

"So that's who you're looking for." He surveyed the buildings as well. He wanted to talk to this sheriff. "When did you last see him?"

"When he took Gypson's body."

"What did he say?"

"That he was looking for you, which cannot be good." Despite his dour words, Vandrill's hold on his Winchester remained relaxed. "One last warning. Leave. You don't want to get involved in the colonel's affairs."

"I'm already involved. Have been since you helped bring Calhoun and his charade to my home and to a town I know better than you."

Vandrill stiffened. "What do you know that I don't?"

"Juniper Flats struggles to keep a doctor and a sheriff. Last time we had either was a year ago."

"Damn." Vandrill's hands tightened around his rifle. "He played me."

"Is our fake sheriff playing Calhoun as well? Or is he your boss' newest hired gun?"

"He's a lawman...of some sort. The best performers pull from the truth."

"And you'd know because you do the same?"

The only indication that Vandrill had heard his question was a slight narrowing of his eyes. "He may not be *this* town's sheriff, but his badge was real."

"What if he stole the badge?"

Using an unfamiliar language, Vandrill growled a lengthy curse that sounded like he was wishing the pox on someone. He scanned the shadows with increased vigor and muttered, "This is what I get for being distracted by a woman."

Surprise, and an uncomfortable surge of jealousy, turned Lewis' voice as surly as a bear whose territory had been invaded. "What woman?"

Vandrill avoided his gaze. "Forget about her. Watch for a big man with—"

"Is this woman Eldora?" Lewis clenched his hands to keep from grabbing hold of Vandrill and shaking the answer out of him.

"*Godverdomme!* You're as bad as Hawk. You're not helping. She's not Mrs. Calhoun. Happy?"

Lewis' tension drained from him like a waterfall.

Vandrill scrubbed his hand over the stubble on his chin. He'd lost not only his ironclad composure but his perfectly groomed appearance as well. "Now, are you going to help or not?"

A new surprise rocked Lewis. "I thought you wanted me to leave."

"I gave you two warnings. I usually don't give any. You've chosen to stay. You might as well be useful."

Lewis nodded. "We're looking for a big man with..." He waited for Vandrill to finish the sentence.

"With a scarred face."

Lewis tried to hold himself still and not react. Could the man be the half-breed Sioux from Nebraska? "What else?"

"He had dark hair and a beard." Vandrill's gaze left the buildings and assessed him. "You know someone who matches that description. No use lying."

Lewis agreed. "Gypson mentioned a scar-faced man."

"I never saw them together."

"But you saw the man before he took Gypson's body?"

"Only once."

He stopped himself from asking, *In Nebraska?* Better to be more ambiguous. "Up north?"

Vandrill's eyes turned sharp as blue frost as he studied Lewis for a long, uncomfortable moment. Finally, he shook his head. "I saw him here in Juniper Flats after I left the colonel at your homestead. He approached me just before I reached town. Told me Gypson knew things others didn't want known, and he'd already organized for someone in the troupe to lookout for the old man."

"He meant Hawk."

"I figured as much. He also said he needed to find a woman who'd left the show."

Lewis' pulse pounded in his veins along with one question: had the man been looking for Eldora or Jane?

"Before you ask, the answer is no. I didn't tell him that Mrs. Calhoun was staying at your cabin."

"Did he give his name?"

"Yeah." Vandrill huffed out a laugh. "John Smith. Should've known then he wasn't being completely honest with me, but I was sidetracked by what came next."

"The woman you mentioned?"

"No," Vandrill snarled. "Have you been listening to anything I said besides that?"

Lewis felt his eyebrows rise in astonishment. Vandrill

was a very long way from the cool and collected man who'd come to his homestead with Calhoun and Eldora a few days ago.

Vandrill spoke through tight lips. "Our devious lawman asked me to help him watch over Gypson."

Lewis eyebrows rose even higher. "Why would he do that? You're Calhoun's thug."

Vandrill's face resumed its blank mask. "I'm many things, but I'm no fool. Smith said a judge named Trafford was coming to Juniper Flats. You keep your eyes on everything when that's about to happen."

"Maybe he was playing you about this Trafford as well. What's so special about him?"

"He's a hanging judge who enjoys digging into the past. Damned badger-like in that respect. If he starts digging 'round you, you'll feel your neck getting itchy. Everyone has something they'd prefer to remain buried."

"How itchy is Calhoun getting?"

Galloping hoofbeats pounded closer.

Vandrill's gaze swung from Lewis to the staging area. He slung the strap of his rifle over his shoulder and let his hands fall to his sides. "You're about to find out."

Calhoun halted his white charger beside Eldora. He glared at Lewis and then Vandrill. Oddly, he didn't seem surprised to see them together. He sent Vandrill a curt nod and urged his horse through the rear flap of the tent.

Vandrill's arm settled around his shoulders. The forced familiarity made him instinctively raise his hands to shrug the man off. Before he could, something jabbed him in the ribs—his own handgun now in Vandrill's other hand. He'd lifted it slick as greased lightning from the holster on Lewis' hip.

"I gave you a chance to leave," Vandrill said in a blasé

tone that, combined with the unreadable expression on his face, told Lewis the man had his emotions locked down again. "Remember that later."

A chill ran up Lewis' spine. "You mean when the judge arrives and digs up my corpse and your sins?"

"Stop focusing on tomorrow if you want to get through the next hour. The colonel has merely asked me to escort you to your seat and keep you there."

"You're not performing tonight?"

"I will be. So will you. We're just waiting for our second cue. But first, we must take our seats." Vandrill's arm tightened around his shoulders, keeping him close so the handgun remained hidden between them as he forced Lewis to walk toward the tent and away from Eldora.

# CHAPTER 10

*I*nside the lofty cathedral of canvas, Calhoun's voice boomed as he introduced his show from the center of the ring. Vandrill guided Lewis along a knee-high barricade that separated the performance area from the audience. Halfway around, he halted in front of two strangers who held pickaxes and mining pans on their laps. They stood and gestured for Vandrill and Lewis to take their seats.

"Aren't we lucky," Vandrill said as they did, and the two men sat on the low wall instead. "Best spot in the tent. You'll be able to see everything from here."

"What am I going to see?" He didn't care what the answer was. All he wanted to see was Eldora.

"The return of Brutus," Vandrill replied.

"Who's that?"

"Our cue. That's when I've been told to set you free. You can join the show or stay on the sidelines and watch. It's your decision."

A brass band struck up a patriotic tune outside, and Calhoun's white charger reared on cue. His front hooves pawed the air as Samson pranced in carrying Eldora. The red, white, and blue ribbons attached to her sidesaddle rippled majestically. The crowd cheered and clapped.

Behind Eldora marched the exuberant quartet, playing a tuba, horn, drum, and cymbals. The string of performers he'd seen assembling outside came next, along with a new addition. The buffalo Eldora had previously mentioned.

Instead of running free, the beast bore a rider and a harness attached to a miniature mountain on a sled. His rider unhooked the contraption in the center of the ring. Then they and everyone, including Eldora and Calhoun, left.

A hush fell over the crowd.

The two miners left their seats on the wall and started singing an upbeat ditty about searching for the legendary El Dorado and its mountains of gold. They strode around the ring, flourishing their pans and pickaxes. One man kept up his energetic pace and the song about getting rich, while the second man slowed, dragging his feet and repeatedly glancing over his shoulder. When the first man paused for breath, the second sang a melancholy tune about leaving his sweetheart Jane and wondering if he'd ever see her again.

"Don't worry," Vandrill reassured him. "We'll all see Eldorado Jane soon."

Suddenly, both miners pretended to see the makeshift mountain for the first time. They shouted "Eureka!" and raced single file up the ramp that led to the top of the mountain.

"Eldorado!" the first man hollered as he jumped into the hole. The second man followed close behind, yelling, "Jane!" Inside the hole, the men's voices echoed, calling, "Eldorado!" and then "Jane!" until their combined voice called, "Where are you, Eldorado Jane?"

"Quite an introduction," Vandrill said as the crowd clapped. "I'm told both Eldora and her friend, Dory, came up with the idea. The two women also choreographed everything that comes next."

As the crowd quieted, digging sounds ensued. Three men crept in wearing long oilskin coats with bandannas over their faces. The murmur of "Outlaws" and "Bandits" rippled through the crowd. Then "watch out" as one of them snuck up the ramp and pointed his pistol down the hole.

The shout of "Eureka!" flew up the hole as did a bag that hit the bandit, forcing him to lower his weapon to catch it. He shook the bag, and it jingled as if full of coins. Two more bags flew out of the hole and were caught by the two bandits on the ground. All three men shook their bags and made them jingle.

The miners in the hole popped out their heads and yelled, "We're rich."

The bandits leveled their pistols at them and replied, "You're dead!"

The miners raised their hands over their heads and cried, "We'll never see Eldorado or Jane again."

A rider dressed entirely in white on a black horse burst through the rear of the tent. Eldora and Samson galloped straight up the ramp. The bandit in front of them threw his bag in the air and dove sideways. Eldora caught the bag, and Samson leapt over the hole. He landed with ease and skidded to a halt directly in front of Lewis.

Eyes wide with disbelief, Eldora stared at him, clearly astonished to see him sitting so close and friendly with Vandrill. He smiled and tipped his hat, hoping to distract her from seeing anything else—namely Vandrill holding him hostage with his own gun. She needed to concentrate on the show and the return of Brutus, whatever or whoever that was.

Unfortunately, his gesture made her frown and study him closer until the crowd's applause claimed her attention. She raised the bag high in acknowledgment.

A chestnut mare with an unusual saddle galloped into the ring. Samson followed the mare seemingly without any direction from Eldora. So this must be the much-missed Delilah.

As the two horses raced around the ring, Eldora hooked her loot bag on Samson's saddle and jumped from him onto Delilah. More bags flew out of the hole. Holding the strategically placed grips on Delilah's saddle, Eldora leaned forward, back, and sideways to catch the bags or scoop them off the ground and then transfer them onto Samson's saddle.

The bandits holstered their pistols and tried to yank her off Delilah. She darted around them. When one got too close, she hit him with a bag and knocked him flat on the ground. He scrambled to the mountain and its shelter.

His cohorts grabbed pickaxes and pans and swung them at her. She snatched a pan from one man's grasp and hit the other over the head with it. Wobbling like a drunkard, he staggered to the mountain and slumped beside his partner.

The final bandit drew his pistol again. Before Lewis could leap to his feet, a shot rang out and Eldora flew backward to lie with her head on Delilah's rump.

She sat up quickly, though, and clutching the horn, she rose to stand on one leg with her other leg straight out behind her. Delilah skidded to a halt beside the shooter, and Eldora swung her leg forward in a dramatic arc to kick him. He did an elaborate fall that included tossing the last bag of gold into the air. Eldora caught it and sat down only long enough to hook both feet in holes on either side of the horn.

As Delilah broke into an easy lope with Samson following her, Eldora rose to stand straight and tall on Delilah's saddle. She opened the bag and threw the glittering contents to the audience.

"Rock candy wrapped in brass foil," Vandrill explained. "The adults love it as much as the children."

When she'd emptied her bag, Eldora halted Delilah in the center of the ring and vaulted down. Samson stopped beside her. She curtsied between the horses while they each bent a foreleg and bowed with her. Lewis found himself clapping just as enthusiastically as the crowd.

"A flawless act," Vandrill said. "But then she's had ten years to refine it to excite both the masses and the elite drawn by Calhoun's heroic name. You won't like what's next even half as much."

"What's that?" Lewis asked.

"The colonel's contribution to the show. It's telling that their creations are so different."

While the crowd continued clapping, the outlaws and miners worked as one to convert the mountain into a bull's-eye target with red and white rings. They took Delilah and left Eldora with only Samson as the hushed beat of Indian drums built to a mighty pounding that filled the tent.

Eldora laid her palm over her heart and gazed around the tent with the exaggerated alarm of an actor. The dread beating in Lewis' heart was real.

A pinto charged in carrying a chief wearing a feathered war bonnet, face paint, and a breastplate full of too many adornments to decipher at his speed. A half-dozen whooping and chanting, bare-chested braves on nimble ponies followed him. When Eldora leapt on Samson, they chased her around the ring.

Vandrill's arm tightened around his shoulder. A handful

of seconds later, the warriors corralled Eldora by the target. "Don't worry. It's part of the act."

The chief pulled Eldora off Samson and into the throng. A loud whoop sounded, and the riders, along with Samson, raced for the exit, revealing Eldora bound with rope to the target. Using long, measured strides, the chief marched away from her. After ten steps, he spun to face her again. This time with his palms raised high.

The drums went silent. So did the crowd. They all stared at the chief, who finally stood still enough for Lewis to see beyond the face paint and war bonnet. The chief was Hawk, and his breastplate contained not only feathers and beads but animal claws.

Claws that could've been used to kill Gypson and make it look like a mountain lion. A reclusive animal that usually stayed far away from towns, even when injured.

Hawk pulled a tomahawk from his belt, widened his stance, and drew back his arm. He aimed the blade at Eldora.

Lewis grabbed the handgun still poking his side and yanked the barrel earthward. He used his other hand to slug Vandrill in the jaw.

The entire time they wrestled for the weapon, Vandrill kept his gaze on the ring. "Stop fighting me and start helping Eldora," he hissed. "Brutus has arrived, and he looks spitting mad. I don't want to shoot him if it can be avoided. So, release the gun and get going." He shoved Lewis toward Eldora. "Your lady needs you."

Vandrill was right. The buffalo that had previously pulled in the mountain-turned-target, now raced around the ring without a rider. Hawk didn't even glance at the buffalo. The Lakota brave's gaze hadn't wavered. Neither had his tomahawk, still raised and ready to throw at Eldora.

Lewis jumped over the wall and raced forward with only his body to protect her.

A SHAGGY BLUR hit the target and slammed it against the back of Eldora's head. Her teeth clacked together. The coppery taste of blood wasn't her biggest concern.

The usually sturdy prop tilted on the verge of tipping over and pinning her beneath its weight—where she could easily be trampled by Brutus. The normally docile buffalo careened around the ring, bellowing in what sounded like pain rather than anger.

She shook off the ropes looped around her wrists. Luckily, they were only there to make the audience believe she couldn't move. She grabbed the sides of the target and heaved backward with all her strength. The target rocked like a bucking bronco before it settled, once more safe and solid against the ground and her spine.

The audience cheered, imagining it was all part of the show.

To the left of the target, something hit the ground with a hefty thunk. The crowd gasped as one, then cheered again. A shiny blade cut the earth while its red and black painted handle vibrated in the air. Behind the familiar tomahawk, Brutus stood frozen, his breath puffing from his nostrils, his hooves sunk in the earth where he'd skidded to a halt to avoid a blade that usually landed in the target next to Eldora's head.

Roy's half of their meticulously-timed show had a loose cog. Brutus wasn't meant to rejoin the show until the grand finale. Why was he here now without a rider or even a saddle? Why did he have a bloody gash on his shoulder? Dread slithered up her spine.

Had Brutus been hurt inside the tent, or had his injury driven him inside?

Whatever the case, he needed to leave before one of their less experienced performers got scared, or pugnacious, and shot him. She eased the tomahawk from the earth and waved it in a wide arc toward the rear of the tent. Brutus' fear made him shuffle back several steps before he glanced in the direction she'd instructed him to go. When he saw the fluttering flap of the exit, he thundered toward it and left the tent.

She longed to follow him, but she wasn't leaving without Lewis. First, she had to find him.

Lewis' seat in the front row was empty. Vandrill was still in his, though. His familiar Winchester lay on his lap along with a revolver she hadn't seen him holding previously. The handgun seemed familiar, but at this distance she wasn't certain why.

The crowd jumped to its feet and roared in appreciation. Vandrill had the audacity to grin at her. Then he gestured with the butt of his rifle toward a spot ten paces from the target, a spot where only Hawk should have stood.

Lewis and Hawk circled each other with their fists raised. Another tomahawk lay on the ground between them. Neither man spoke. They didn't take their eyes off each other either.

"Give 'm 'ell, Adams!"

"Yeah! Don't let him throw any more blades at the lady."

She'd forgotten the crowd was made up of Lewis' neighbors. She raced toward him. She also adjusted her grip on the tomahawk, preparing to throw it if Hawk or Vandrill or anyone pointed a weapon at Lewis.

When Hawk saw her coming, he lowered his fists and his voice as well, so the crowd couldn't hear. "He tried to tackle me as I threw my warning blade at Brutus."

"He was throwing at you," Lewis growled.

She picked up the second tomahawk lying between them in case either man decided to use it. "Hawk was just doing his job."

Lewis raised an eyebrow at her soothing tone. He knew she was trying to placate him.

She was also trying to keep her voice from carrying to the audience. "You shouldn't be fighting."

Hawk shrugged. "I wasn't. I was keeping him occupied till you arrived and calmed him down. Today I have many jobs."

"Wasn't one of them to protect her father?" Lewis snarled. "Look how that turned out."

Hawk's customary calm vanished. Rage reddened his face. His fingers clenched and his muscles bunched, preparing to throw a real punch. Before he could, the clear notes of a bugle echoed in the tent.

The call for the final act had come early. With the show's current disruptions, the call shouldn't have come at all.

Roy's voice boomed, announcing the Battle of the Little Big Horn, calling it a heroic but ill-fated battle provoked by a heathen treachery. Their reenactment took on a whole new meaning now that she knew Roy's past in Nebraska.

A handful of mounted men wearing pristine blue uniforms and brandishing shining sabers charged into the tent. Eldora grabbed Hawk's arm and jerked him toward Lewis.

Lewis gaped at her in disbelief. "What are you doing?"

She turned her back to him and spun Hawk around to

do the same. "We're forming a triangle, so we won't get trampled."

"Or stabbed in the back with a saber," Hawk added. "If you haven't noticed, odd things are happening in this show."

Hawk sounded calm again. She prayed he'd stay that way. She'd never seen him so angry as when Lewis mentioned his failure to help her father. Her life was once again spiraling into bedlam. A flash of black and white joined the swarm running circles around them. Hawk's pinto had returned to the ring.

"My ride's here," Hawk said. "Better call yours."

She raised her fingers to her lips. Before she could whistle, Samson burst through the rear of the tent. Eldora signaled for him to stop beside her rather than race past for a running mount. She'd leave with Lewis or not at all.

A second after Samson halted, Lewis scooped her up and threw her on Samson. She dropped the tomahawks and grabbed his arm to help him jump up behind her. Then she urged Samson toward the exit.

Hawk was already racing that way. He made his escape. Samson did not. The cavalry jostled them into another circuit around the arena before he broke free.

The cool air outside the tent filled Eldora with relief. She drew in a deep breath and relaxed—until Lewis' body slammed against her.

His arms tightened around her for a split second, then he let go. He fell off Samson and disappeared into the darkness beyond the brightly lit tent. He landed with a crash that sounded like wood splintering.

Eldora leapt off Samson and felt her way through the murky rabbit warren of crates that made up the staging area. Occasional streams of light cast by the big tent helped her search. Otherwise, she hunted by moonlight.

By touch. In silence. Too afraid to speak. As soon as she touched the crates reduced to kindling, she also found Lewis.

The panic gripping her chest only eased when she grabbed his hand and he squeezed back.

"Can you stand?"

He grunted. "Not without your help."

Inside the tent, the crowd continued cheering. They still assumed everything they saw was part of an act. The grim truth weighed heavily on her. So did Lewis as she wedged her shoulder under his arm and shoved him onto his feet.

He staggered, and his breath hissed between his teeth.

When she looped her arm around his back to steady him, her hand slipped on something wet and warm. "You're bleeding. Someone shot you!"

"They threw a knife at me." He wrapped her fingers around the hilt of a knife.

"You pulled it out?"

"It's the only weapon we have, so you'd better hold on to it. I would, but I'm feeling a mite dizzy."

The blur and whistle of something flying over her head made her duck. Lewis did the same. A knife lodged in the crate above them.

"Still believe you can trust Hawk?" Lewis whispered.

She pushed Lewis away from where the knife had been thrown. "This isn't Hawk," she replied in an equally hushed voice. "If it were, we'd already be dead."

Behind them someone crashed into a crate and uttered a muffled curse.

"All right," Lewis muttered. "Our knifeman isn't light on his feet. He isn't Hawk, but he's working with him."

"You can't know for sure." She kept pushing him away from the sound of their attacker fumbling in the dark.

Whoever he was, they were very lucky he wasn't *light on his feet*.

"Hawk left the tent ahead of us." Lewis kept his voice so low she had to strain to hear him. "Now he's nowhere to be seen, but I hear the tread of his moccasins circling us. They're working together." Lewis' knees buckled and his weight bore her to the ground.

She managed to shove him behind a stack of crates before they both fell on their sides. When she reached for him again, the back of his shirt was drenched in blood.

Fear made her hands shake as she ripped the overskirt from her costume and pressed it to his wound. "Rest for a moment while I stop your bleeding."

"No time," he said from between clenched teeth as he hauled himself into a sitting position and leaned his shoulder against the crates. "I'll draw their attention while you run for the tent and help."

"I'm not leaving you."

"You can't stay. Hawk's costume has more claws than a cat."

"You think—" Eldora shook her head. "Hawk's breast-plate has bear claws."

"That could've been used to kill your father. We'll only know for sure if we get a chance to examine his wounds."

First, they had to escape their attacker. His boots scuffed the dirt, coming closer until they fell silent on the other side of the crates. She held her breath. In the hush, she finally heard the second pair of footsteps, moving so softly their owner must be wearing moccasins. Lewis was right. Two men stalked them.

"Get ready to run," he whispered and then shouted, "Come any closer and you're dead! I have Eldora's derringer."

She wished he did. Unfortunately, she'd left it behind after changing into her costume. Silence followed Lewis' bluff.

She decided to add her own. "We know it's you, Roy," she yelled. "If we're wrong, then you can only be Robert Wardell."

"How do you know that name?" Roy roared from the other side of the crates.

Lewis shoved her sideways as the crates exploded like they'd been head-butted by Brutus. The knife flew from her hand. The crates hit Lewis and sent him flying as well. He landed flat on his back with Roy on top of him.

She scrambled to find the knife. Her fingers brushed the splintered end of a broken crate slat. She snatched it up, intending to stab Roy and shove him off Lewis.

The hunched silhouette of Roy pressing her tiny derringer against Lewis' forehead stopped her.

The white of Roy's teeth flashed in the moonlight as he snarled. "The only man who will die tonight is you, Mr. Adams."

"Kill him and you'll have to kill me as well."

"No!" Lewis shouted. "Run! I want you to live. I love you."

His declaration, so swift and certain, filled her with her own conviction. "I love you as well. More than my life. I'll *never* leave you."

Roy gaped at her. "You want to stay with this boring backwoods farmer *forever*?" He nodded as if it were for the best. "So be it. You shall both die tonight."

Shock numbed her brain. She strove for the words to reason with him.

"My dear, distraught wife," Roy drawled in a snide tone. "Do not be so heartbroken. Your deaths will be quick, which is more than you deserve." He held the derringer firm against Lewis' head as he leaned toward her. "Your adulterous affair is over. All that's left is your final performance. The script reads: you shot your lover and used your derringer to end your shame."

"You can't kill us," she repeated. "You'll lose my act and whatever's left of your show to scandal."

"You've already killed my show." Roy's voice went flat with resignation. "You deserve to die with it."

"No one will believe Eldora is a killer," Lewis said. "They'll hang you for murder."

Roy's gaze swung from her to Lewis. "Not murder. Self-preservation. Not my fault!" His hand shook as he pressed the derringer harder against Lewis' forehead.

Clasping her makeshift weapon in both hands, Eldora raised the stake over her head. Only one thing mattered. Saving Lewis. If Roy saw her about to stab him, he'd turn the derringer her way. She might strike a hit before he shot her. Either way, she'd give Lewis a chance.

Before she could, Lewis asked, "Is that what you told yourself in Nebraska?"

"Nebraska," Roy said, drawing out the word like a curse. "That's how you know Wardell's name. He invited me to Dodge under the pretense of funding my show, but he spoke only of Nebraska and blackmail."

She tightened her grip on her stake. What could she say to entice Roy to look her way? He wanted to defeat Wardell. "I know Wardell's—"

"You know nothing," Roy snarled. "Wardell's demands kept growing. I kept paying. For another act not my fault."

"I know his weakness." She didn't, but it was her best bluff. "You can use it to blackmail Wardell."

Behind her, the click of a large weapon being cocked

echoed softly. She'd hesitated too long. She'd lost her only chance. Vandrill and his Winchester had arrived to help his boss.

But he hadn't. Instead, a scar-faced bear of a man loomed over her with a sawed-off shotgun.

"You can drop your stick, miss. I've got this." For such a big man, his moccasin-clad feet made very little noise as he stepped closer to Roy.

She kept a tight grip on her crate slat.

The man didn't seem to notice or care. His gaze remained on Roy. "You're responsible for your own actions, Calhoun. So am I." He set his double-barreled shotgun against the back of Roy's skull. "I couldn't stop you from committing murder twenty-four years ago, but I will today." His voice lowered to a guttural snarl. "Keep holding onto that peashooter. Give me a reason to blast you back to hell."

Roy dropped her derringer and raised his hands in the air. "This is all a misunderstanding, Mr. Smith. I was bluffing. I never intended to kill them. I only wished to scare my wife into obedience."

Eldora dropped her stake so she could retrieve her derringer instead and aim it at Roy as well. "Get your lying ass off Lewis."

Smith poked Roy's head with his shotgun. "Do as the lady says. Move real slow, or my finger might slip on the trigger." As soon as Roy complied, Smith sent him sprawling with a fierce, flatfooted kick to his backside. "Stay on your stomach with your hands behind your head. Make sure you face away from the lady. She doesn't need to see your ugly mug any longer."

"My lawyer is inside the tent." Roy's voice, although muffled by the ground, grew stronger, confident that he could talk his way out of this. "Fetch him, and he will explain everything."

Smith snorted a laugh. "Vandrill can join us under his own steam."

"You know him! If you do, you also know you should release me now and—"

"You're not going anywhere. So button your lip and stop annoying me with your jabbering!" Smith drew in a long breath and then glanced at her. "Did you get hurt in the scuffle, miss?" he asked in a considerably gentler tone than he'd used with Roy.

She shook her head.

"Then you'd best stow that derringer and tend to Mr. Adams' injury." He pulled a bandanna from his pocket and tossed it to her. "Use that to help stop his bleeding. You don't need to worry about Calhoun any longer."

She tucked the derringer into her belt and rolled Lewis onto his side so she could press the bandanna against his wound. The small strip of cloth turned sodden in seconds. She ripped off one leg of her trousers and laid it over the bandanna. She sent a silent thank you heavenward that the legs of her costume were so wide. Every inch of fabric might be needed to save Lewis' life. She sent up a prayer for that outcome as well.

"Handsome John?" Lewis squinted up at their savior. "Am I hallucinating?"

"You ain't, but you look pale enough to be a specter in some hellish nightmare. Sorry this spawn of Satan got you before I could get him."

The rigid muscles along Lewis' back relaxed. "Sadie always said you knew how to save the day at the last minute."

Smith shifted his feet as if uncomfortable. "Mrs. Ballantyne only remembers the good, not the bad."

"Heard you've been calling yourself John Smith," Lewis said. "That your real name?"

"Judge Trafford gave it to me. My only other name is a Sioux name...if you don't count Madam Garrett christening me Handsome John when I worked for her in Dodge."

To Eldora, the man would always be an angel. "Thank you for saving us."

Smith's gaze remained on Roy as he gave her a curt nod. "Glad I could help. Need to make up for a few bad turns in the road I took. One being Dodge."

"That why you impersonated Juniper Flats' sheriff?" Lewis asked.

Disbelief made her gasp. "You're the man who took my father's body. Why?"

Light steps approached at a run. So did a swaying orb of light.

Smith kept his gaze and his shotgun on Roy. "Best if I answer your questions after Hawk hog-ties Calhoun and we get Mr. Adams some medical attention."

Hawk ran out of the dark, carrying a lantern.

"What took you so long, little brother?" Concern resonated in John's voice.

"Had trouble finding these." Hawk held up the lantern and a coil of rope.

More footsteps approached, slightly heavier than but equally as swift as Hawk's had been.

Hawk and John moved lightning fast. Hawk planted his knee between Roy's shoulder blades and pinned him to the ground while John swung his shotgun toward whoever approached.

Vandrill halted with his hands in the air. "It's just me."

"I see that now," Smith said. "I also see you're holding a revolver and a Winchester."

When Vandrill lowered them, Smith turned his shotgun on Roy again. "You'd best announce your approach till I get familiar with the sound of your boots, Vandrill."

"Mr. Vandrill!" Roy gushed with relief. "I require your help. There has been a grave misunderstanding."

Smith grunted. "If you want to help with Calhoun's *misunderstanding*, take the lantern from Hawk and see how Mr. Adams and the lady are doing."

"He works for me, not you," Roy said in his imperious voice. "He will assist me first. Gather my troupe, Mr. Vandrill, and bring them to me so we can—"

"You've cooked your own goose, Calhoun." Vandrill grabbed the lantern. "I cannot help you anymore. Not sure anyone can."

"Y-you—You coward!" Roy sputtered. "A good lawyer never quits."

"Time you learned I'm neither good nor a lawyer. I'm merely lucky to find someone who showed me enough to pose as a lawyer. Only helpful thing he did."

"Advice can be as helpful as action." Hawk tied Roy's hands behind his back and recited, "*No person shall be deprived of life, liberty, or property, without due process of law.*"

"You heathen traitor!" Roy snarled over his shoulder. "The law is with me. You all work for me."

Hawk sighed. "You'll make a fine witness against yourself."

"Release me or I will ensure you never work again!"

"Too bad your husband won't listen to Hawk's counsel and be silent," Vandrill muttered as he crouched beside Eldora and shone his light on Lewis' makeshift bandages.

The blood staining them bright red made her send

another prayer heavenward and tear off her remaining trouser leg.

"Adams needs a doctor." Vandrill's eyes narrowed as he caught her gaze.

She shook her head. "Juniper Flats doesn't have a doctor. It doesn't matter. He'll be fine without one." She pressed the second leg of her costume over the first. "I'll tend to his wounds."

"Eldora, you need help. You're running out of..." Lewis' voice faded into an unintelligible jumble of slurred words.

Worry made her lean so close to him that her nose brushed his cheek. "I'm running out of what?" she prompted.

"Cloth, of course."

His answer made her smile.

"I love making you smile," he whispered. "I'd love to see you naked as well. Just not right now. So tell Vandrill to bring you more cloth before you strip yourself bare trying to help me. Tell him to give back my handgun, too."

She jerked her head up so she could glare at Vandrill. "You lowdown cur! How was he supposed to protect himself if you took—?"

"Berate me later." Vandrill handed the revolver to her. "I'm off to fetch that cloth he mentioned." He scooped up the lantern and disappeared along with its light, leaving her alone in the dark with John and Hawk's voices fading in and out as they discussed what to do with Roy.

Lewis' murmur broke through.

She bowed her head to better hear him again. "What did you say?"

He grasped her hand. "Stay with me, Angel Eyes." His drawl had deepened into a rasping rumble.

She held his hand tight and continued pressing her

other hand against his wound. She let her tears fall unchecked.

Lewis' fingers brushed her cheek and his voice went even hoarser. "Eldora—"

"I want you to know my real name." She leaned down on her elbow so she could face him. The earth brushed hard and unforgiving against her cheek as she kissed him softly and whispered, "I'm Dorothy. Dorothy Gypson."

He explored her lips with a tender kiss. "Good name, but you'll always be my Angel Eyes or maybe my..." His smile grew into a mischievous grin. "My Dory."

She managed a tearful laugh. "That's what Jane made me call her. So I made her call me Doro."

He laughed as well and then winced. "She's a devil of a best friend. I'm glad she found you and kept you safe until you could come back to Juniper Flats, and me. I was mighty happy when I heard you were no longer married. I want to call you by another name, *my wife*."

"You will, because I'm not letting anyone touch you again. Even if there was a doctor here, I wouldn't trust him to stitch you up. I'll do it on my own."

"You're not alone." Despite his words his voice drew hushed and slurred again. "We have friends at the Ballantyne Ranch."

"It's too dark to see those glossy-green cedar elms you told me about. I won't find where to turn on the trail." She grasped his hand tighter. "You must stay awake and show me."

When he didn't reply, she shook him. "Promise me you'll stay awake and show me."

He nodded. "I will. After that we'll depend on Lila. She'll make a beeline for the Ballantyne's house, or more precisely their barn."

"It's a long ride." He'd lose more blood along the way. Too much. Her heart raced with fear, but she made sure her voice remained calm. "Where's Lila?"

"At the livery. So we'll have to ask John to help us again. Ask him to retrieve Lila and then ask him for one last thing —help getting me up onto her saddle. Then the race is on."

"I'll whistle for Samson and be right behind you."

"Not for long." His soft chuckle caressed her ears. "But I bet you and Samson can't get ahead of us. I won't slow down, but I still want you by my side until we reach the Ballantyne Ranch." He paused to draw in a slow breath. "Before we go, there's another thing I need."

"Whatever you need, it's yours."

"Will you kiss me again? For luck?"

She kissed him with all her heart, all her love and passion and hope as well. Because despite Lewis' promise to stay awake, and his bet that he could ride as fast as her, and his desire to stay by her side until they reached the Ballantyne Ranch—his bleeding hadn't stopped. This might be their last kiss.

# CHAPTER 11

*L*ewis jolted awake. Lying face down on his stomach, his entire body hurt like the devil.

A heavy hand landed on his shoulder and held him still while a lighter hand poked the wound on his back. The shadows circling the light above his head pulsed inward with every jab of what felt like a needle. Pain. Confusion. Guilt. They came in waves, threatening to drown him in a dark oblivion.

He clutched the edge of the wood plank beneath him in an effort to stay awake. He'd broken his promise to Eldora. He'd passed out. Where was he? More importantly, where was Eldora?

When the hands retreated, so did his pain. It ebbed to a throbbing knot, waiting to torment him again.

Eldora's soothing voice caressed his ears. "I'm sorry I keep causing you pain."

Relief washed over him. Eldora was still with him. "You're the best thing that ever rode into my life." He'd aimed for a comforting tone, but his words came out gruff, like a bear fighting the lure of hibernation.

"The worst is over. I've finished stitching your wound. The bleeding's stopped."

"You sure you're done?" Perversely, he hoped not. He wanted to feel her touch again.

"You can sleep in a moment," she said. "After we wrap bandages around your waist."

That sounded good...except for the "we." He raised his head enough to see what lay beneath him. The Ballantyne's kitchen table. Noah and Sadie couldn't be far.

Sure enough, Noah's steady hand grasped his arm. "You've relaxed long enough. Eldora told us you've been dozing ever since you made the turnoff. She had to tie you to Lila to get you here. Time to get up." Noah easily lifted him to sit upright on the edge of the table.

So easily, there was no need for Eldora to touch him again. Disappointment joined his aches and pains. He had to stop falling off horses.

He tried to concentrate on his troubles beyond the night-shrouded room. Find Jane. Protect Eldora. Make sure Calhoun was in jail. Ask Handsome John how he knew Calhoun. Tell Noah and Sadie the man who'd helped make her a prisoner in Dodge was now in Juniper Flats posing as its sheriff.

The devil surely had a hand in that as well. The shadows tormented his vision again. He clutched the table on either side of him and focused on just staying upright.

Behind him, the pad of bare feet came closer and stopped.

"Hang in there," Sadie said. "When the bandaging is finished, you can sleep again. Right now you need that more than anything else."

His vision cleared enough to see Sadie standing beside him with her red hair flowing long and loose over her night wrapper and gown. She cradled a roll of white linen while Noah held a lantern over him and his two nurses. The same unwavering light that had helped Eldora finish her stitching.

He blinked his heavy-lidded eyes, struggling to keep his saviors in focus. "I'm sorry we disturbed you in the middle of the night."

"Nonsense," Sadie said as she handed Eldora one end of his bandages. "I would've been *disturbed* if I'd learned later that you hadn't come."

"I don't know what I'd have done without your help." The worry lines on Eldora's pale face faded as she smiled at Sadie.

The sight of Eldora's relief eased his fatigue as well. So did the warmth of her fingers brushing his bare skin as she wrapped the cloth around his waist. His entire body stiffened with the desire to have her touch a helluva lot more of him.

Eldora's smile vanished, probably thinking she was causing him more pain. "What kind of town doesn't have a doctor?" Her tone had turned outraged on his behalf.

"We have trouble enticing doctors to our community, but none at all getting famous Wild West shows to visit." He winked at her and was rewarded with the return of her smile.

"Stop teasing Eldora," Sadie said in a motherly tone that failed to conceal her amusement. "She asks an excellent question. One I've voiced many times as well." She sighed. "We hoped Doctor Rhodes might fill the position, but he remains in Dodge."

"Other than Marshal Masterson," Noah muttered, "Rhodes is the only one from Dodge I'd welcome."

Eldora sent Lewis a worried glance before asking, "There's no one else from Dodge you'd welcome?"

She was testing the waters for the best way to handle the news of Handsome John being in town.

"No one." Noah's tone was hard as granite.

Sadie helped Eldora tie off Lewis' bandages. "We're done."

"Thank you," Lewis said. "With you three taking such good care of me, I never needed a doctor. But we could still use a marshal. Any chance Masterson's nearby?"

Noah shrugged. "Last I heard he was in Dodge, but that doesn't mean he's still there."

Very true. Lewis' thoughts spun with the conundrum named Handsome John Smith until Eldora's yawn snared his attention. He yearned to hold her in his arms as they both fell asleep. That way, when she woke up rested in the morning, he could immediately kiss her and—

The light around him flared along with his desire.

Sadie set a second lantern on the table beside him. "Eldora and Lewis need some privacy." She clasped her husband's hand and tried to tug him, and the light he held, away from the table. "They also need clean clothes. Let's go to our room and retrieve some."

Noah didn't budge. "I haven't heard who stabbed Lewis." His eyes narrowed as he studied him. "I'm wondering why."

"Our guests need to talk without us hovering over them." Sadie grasped Noah's chin and turned him to face her. "So do we. Come with me. Now."

Lewis felt his eyebrows rise in wonder over Sadie's unusual abruptness.

As soon as they left, Eldora leaned close to him and whispered, "What's Noah got against Mr. Smith?"

"He forced Sadie to live and work in a saloon in Dodge. It was also a brothel."

Eldora's eyes widened with disbelief.

"We need to return to town before John comes here looking for us."

"If Noah sees him—" She pressed her lips tight. "I've done enough doctoring tonight." Her gaze dropped to her clothes.

His blood stained the previously pristine white costume, from her chest to a ragged line above her knees—where the rest of the outfit had been torn free to save his life.

"What if I hadn't been able to save you?"

"But you did. I couldn't ask for a better partner." How could he ask her to leave the safety of this house and journey with him into the unknown? "Only one of us needs to return to town."

Her gaze locked with his. "We're stronger together. And if we are truly partners, we will act together."

Her determination made him smile. He nodded. "In harmony, like Jane said."

His words sparked her glorious smile. A smile so bright it shone in her eyes.

"And like how Sadie and Noah act." A tiny frown marred her happiness as she glanced at their door. "They've been gone a while, haven't they?"

They'd been gone longer than seemed necessary to find a change of clothing for him and Eldora. "Been awfully quiet as well."

The door to their room burst open. It hit the wall with a startling bang. Noah stomped back to the table, followed by a very worried-looking Sadie. So much for harmony.

"Sadie believes—" Noah halted to hold out his arm, and Sadie slipped into his embrace. They stood united again.

Even their grim expressions matched. "Sadie believes Wardell stabbed you, and he's coming after me next."

Lewis rushed to reassure them. "Calhoun attacked me. When I last saw him, he was in the law's custody."

"Then why did you natter on about people from Dodge instead of telling us that? You mentioned everyone except —" Noah's arm tightened around Sadie.

Sadie hugged him back and finished the sentence for him. "Wardell."

Eldora moved closer and grasped Lewis' hand.

He drew strength from her steadfast support. "The town's sheriff, who came to our rescue, is from Dodge."

Noah rubbed a weary hand over his eyes. "You're a terrible liar."

"Yes, he is," Eldora replied. "But he isn't lying now. Neither am I. The man who rescued us could be a worthwhile ally."

"You mean this mysterious sheriff?" Noah heaved a sigh. "Juniper Flats doesn't have one."

"Handsome John is here," Lewis blurted.

"We left him in Juniper Flats," Eldora added just as quickly, "where he's been impersonating the sheriff."

Noah and Sadie gaped at them in shocked silence.

"Well..." Sadie said. "That's not so bad. Better John than Wardell."

Ignoring Wardell wouldn't keep his friends safe. "I hate to say this, but Wardell is probably nearby as well. Calhoun confirmed he's the blackmailer who wants my land and most likely your water."

"He wants Sadie as well." Noah pulled a matching pair of hunting rifles from a rack above the mantel and handed one to Sadie.

Her freckles lay stark against her suddenly pale face as

she clutched the rifle to her chest. "Wardell didn't leave his obsession in Dodge like we'd hoped."

Noah pressed a firm kiss against her forehead. "This isn't Dodge. You're safe here. Lewis and Eldora will stay with you while I see how many of our men have returned from the roundup. We'll all keep a lookout for Wardell. And John. I don't trust him."

Outside the house, a horse whinnied.

"More of your men returning?" Lewis asked hopefully.

Noah shook his head. "That's coming from the barn."

The whinny sounded again. This time shrill with warning.

"That's Samson!" Eldora's voice plummeted to a whisper. "He heard something."

Everyone inside the house went still as statues, straining to hear more.

"One rider approaching fast." Lewis reached for his gun belt, still strapped to his hips. His fingers curled into a fist when he found it empty.

"Too fast. Trouble's coming." Eldora crossed to a sideboard and returned with his handgun and Henry rifle.

He accepted the rifle but refused the handgun. "Remember, you need something bigger than your derringer out here." He kissed her cheek to reassure her, and because she stood too close to resist.

"Too dark to see who's outside." Noah had crossed to peer out the window to the left of the front door.

Sadie stood close behind him, doing the same. "Lewis, douse the lanterns so they won't see us either."

After he did, they all stood stock-still, listening in the dark silence within to the hoofbeats growing louder outside—until they halted a short distance from the porch.

"Hello in the house," a man called without delay, but also in a cordial tone. "I come in peace."

Noah frowned over his shoulder at Sadie. "That sounds like—" He inhaled sharply and yelled, "That had better not be you, Handsome John."

"And if it is?"

"You should've stayed in Juniper Flats. Or even better in Dodge!"

John's voice maintained its affable tone. "I come in peace," he repeated.

"He shouldn't have come at all," Noah grumbled.

Sadie laid a hand on his arm. "He helped me once."

Noah's reply came quick. "What about all the other times when he didn't?"

"He's the only reason Lewis and I are alive." When Eldora crept across the room to the other window flanking the door, he followed close. Not even his wound, complaining with every step, stopped him from being her shadow.

On the other side of the glass, all remained dark.

"Still not sure we should trust him. Not completely." Lewis glanced at Sadie and Noah, who continued to stare out the other window. "When we departed Juniper Flats, we left too many unanswered questions."

"Well, then it's time he answers them," Sadie replied in a hushed but determined voice. Then she yelled, "Tell us why you're here, John."

"Mrs. Ballantyne." John sounded pleased to recognize her voice. He continued in a contrite tone. "I apologize for coming uninvited to your home in the middle of the night, but it's better if I finish my conversation with Mr. Adams and his friend while you and Mr. Ballantyne are present. We all have a mutual enemy in Robert Wardell."

"Since when is he your adversary?" Noah shouted.

"Since twenty-four years ago."

"If you're the boy who survived the Sioux reservation massacre, why not kill your enemies?" Lewis asked.

"I've been told I should seek justice instead."

"Justice?" Noah scoffed. "You worked for Wardell in Dodge."

"A necessary evil."

"And Madam Garrett?"

"Another. She claimed she knew secrets about everyone in Dodge. I had to earn her trust to learn what she knew, but it wasn't enough."

"Enough what?" Eldora asked.

"Proof. I needed evidence that Wardell was a killer. I knew he played a role in my mother's death. In Nebraska, I'd been told he was the Indian agent responsible for my people's starvation. I suspected he'd lined up the players to silence us."

Calhoun and his insubordinate soldiers. Wardell had controlled Calhoun even back then. "Where's the colonel now?"

"The town might not have a doctor or a sheriff, but it has a fine jail—and Hawk to guard it.

"He works for you?"

"We work together. Hawk has kept me apprised of what's been happening in Calhoun's show. Now that Calhoun's behind bars, he's talking to me as well."

Roy hadn't taken Hawk's advice to remain silent.

"What if he's lying?" Eldora asked.

"Doesn't matter. I have what I need. Calhoun fell into my trap. He'll be charged with attempted murder and the intent to commit another. He was seen trying to stab and shoot Mr.

Adams and overheard saying he'd kill Miss Gypson. My gamble paid off."

Fury rocked Lewis. John had gambled with Eldora's life. "You disrupted the show. You wanted Calhoun to panic and do something desperate. All to get the proof necessary for any type of murder charge. You used us as bait."

"A necessary evil," John replied in a flat tone devoid of emotion.

"You used Sadie as well." Noah's words rumbled with the anger Lewis felt. "You'll burn in hell."

"I already do. Every day."

"I'm sorry," Eldora called out to John. She used her familiar soft, soothing tone. "I apologize for the murder of your mother and your people."

A stunned silence on both sides of the wall followed.

"Why?" The incredulity in John's shout made Lewis flinch. "Why do *you* apologize? They aren't your sins."

"My father regretted his role in the tragedy. I speak for him."

"I—" John paused as if he struggled with some internal demon. When he spoke again, his voice was so hoarse he almost wasn't understandable. "I apologize as well. Many times I wanted to kill your father and nearly did. Calhoun and Wardell as well."

"What stopped you?" Lewis asked. They'd be wise to learn what controlled a man like John.

"Judge Trafford."

"The hanging judge? You feared he'd dig up your past?"

"Nothing there Trafford doesn't already know." John sounded amused and sad at the same time. "After I fled from the reservation, I ran into Hawk. We banded together to survive and stole what we needed till Trafford caught us and gave us a choice. Do time in jail or work for him. I became the law's hand and Hawk, its head. He knows enough to be a lawyer. Too bad he'll never be one. I must leave now."

John's abrupt announcement made Eldora gasp. He reached out to comfort her at the same time she reached for the window.

She pressed her palm against the glass as if to stop John. "Where are you going?"

"Calhoun claims he found your father's body before Hawk and Vandrill did," John replied.

When Eldora stiffened, Lewis laid his hand over hers on the window, wanting to remind her she wasn't alone. "On the trail leading to my homestead?" he asked.

"No, in Gypson's old caravan...killed by his own shotgun."

Eldora jerked away from the glass as if it had cut her. She turned her palm to thread her fingers with Lewis' and held on tight. "My father would never shoot himself."

"Calhoun said the same. He also said Wardell murdered your father and left his body as a test. He moved it to the trail, dug out the shells and turned the holes into slashes with a claw he removed from Hawk's costume."

Eldora drew in a sharp breath. "Wardell made Roy orchestrate another performance. A death from a mountain lion attack. He showed he was still Wardell's puppet. But he's yours now. Wardell can no longer pull Roy's strings to get what he wants."

"So he'll go after others he thinks he can control," John replied.

Eldora's muscles went rigid. "You mean me."

"You are surrounded by three friends who, if I'm not mistaken, are well armed. Wardell will attempt to draw you out of your safe haven by going after your friend Dory."

Eldora surged toward the door. Lewis maintained his

hold on her hand to keep her from rushing outside and confronting their dubious ally.

When she tried to twist out of his grasp, he pulled her flat against his chest and kept her there with his arm around her waist. "I can't let you go."

Her eyes glittered in the dark as she gazed up at him. "John's going after Jane." Her voice broke and her tears fell. "He'll watch and wait for Wardell to grab her."

"I can't let you offer yourself up as bait instead. We'll find another way. We'll work together to save her."

"I'm sorry, Miss Gypson." John's voice faded, growing more distant. He was leaving. "I will try to keep your friend safe."

But unlike him and Eldora, that wouldn't be John's first priority. Eldora slumped against him. She hid her face and her grief against his chest, but she kept a tight hold on his revolver—as she had since John arrived.

# CHAPTER 12

"*T*hought he'd never leave," Noah muttered.

Hanging onto Lewis and his revolver, Eldora contemplated her options for leaving as well. When she lifted her head from his chest, the first thing she saw was Noah and Sadie standing together, his arm looped around her shoulders, her face turned up to his, smiling. They made a perfect replica of the tintype of Noah's parents on the mantel.

Then, acting in harmony, they turned as one to face her and Lewis.

"John won't go far," Noah said in a reassuring tone. "He needs sleep as much as we do."

Sadie nodded. "And in the morning there will be no talk of anyone going anywhere alone, or even the two of you riding off without our help."

"The four of us will work together," Noah said, "to save Jane."

Sadie glanced at the window. "The five of us."

"You put too much faith in John." Noah ran a tired hand over his eyes again.

"He'll help us." Eldora paused and then added. "If he can."

Lewis' lips brushed her hair in a soft caress. "In the morning, we can add two more to our numbers. We'll ride to my family's ranch. Oralee and Olivia will help."

"Your sisters!" Worry raised her gaze to meet his. "If something happens to you and Jane, Oralee and Olivia will inherit the Dority land and be next in Wardell's sights."

Lewis tenderly tucked her mussed hair behind her ears. "They'll be all right as long as they stick together and stay close to home until we find Jane."

"Sadie..." A worried note rumbled in Noah's voice. "When we get to the Adams Ranch—"

Sadie cut him off. "I know. I must stay with Olivia and Oralee in order to have the best chance of keeping Jacob safe."

Noah pulled his wife into a fierce hug. "With the Adams sisters on your side, you'll all be safe."

Sadie hugged him back just as tightly. "And you'll be able to concentrate on making your way back to us."

Noah stared over his wife's head at them. "I'll ride with you. Together we'll find Jane."

Eldora felt her eyes widen. "You'd leave your family for Jane and me?"

"I'm leaving to protect my family." Noah's grim smile softened. "This includes you, since I'm guessing Lewis wants to marry you. His family is my family."

Eldora had daydreamed about the Ballantyne and Adams families for a very long time. To suddenly be given the chance to become one of them was dizzying.

Sadie slipped out of her husband's embrace and pulled her from Lewis'. She guided her across the room, picking up and lighting the lantern as they went. "Let me show you where you can sleep."

As tired as she was, she wanted something more than sleep. She wanted Lewis. She yearned to see his expression, to know if he wanted the same thing.

His footsteps followed close, but then so did Noah's. Sadie opened the door to a small but tidy room with a trunk at the foot of a bed covered in a patchwork quilt.

"There's another empty bedroom next to this one," Noah said. "Maybe Lewis should use it so Eldora doesn't have to... listen to his snoring."

Sadie laughed. "I knew this day would come."

"What day is that?"

"The day you began teasing Lewis as much as he teases you and me, and the rest of his family."

"It's fun, and turnabout is fair play."

Lewis' sigh sounded not only tired but tense. "Could we move this fun along? Eldora still needs a nightgown and a clean dress for the morning."

"Oh, yes. Don't go anywhere until I get them. I've got more opinions on the sleeping arrangements."

Sadie drew her close and whispered, "Don't worry. As soon as Noah returns, we'll leave you and Lewis to decide what's best." She moved into the room and hung the lantern on a hook beside the bed. "One day this room, or the one next door, will be Jacob's. For now, he's staying with us at the other end of the house. So both rooms are free and you can do whatever you like."

Noah returned with a pile of clothing, a pitcher of water, and a basin. He set them all on the trunk. "Thought you might like to clean up before you don your new clothing. Now about the sleeping arrangements—" He grabbed Sadie's hand and tugged her out of the room. "Have fun figuring them out. We'll close this door, so you don't have to."

As the door closed behind them, Eldora glimpsed Sadie flinging her arms around Noah's neck and hugging him. Eldora wanted to hug both of them for their kindness and for leaving her alone with Lewis.

He stood near the foot of the bed, frowning at it. "I need to tell you something."

His grim tone made her brow furrow as well. She perched on the edge of the mattress, making sure to leave enough space for him to sit beside her.

Instead, he sat on the trunk, much too far away and looking everywhere but at her. "You've every right not to trust me after how I behaved toward your father in his caravan."

She moved to the foot of the mattress. "I trust you even more after that."

"How could you?"

She fought the urge to touch him. Lewis needed words as well as actions. "You pointed a gun at my father, but you didn't use it. Not even when he pestered you like a...what did you call him? A royal jackass." She smiled at that part of the memory.

Lewis' face remained solemn. "He was a good father."

*Yes, he was. And now he's gone. I can't lose you as well.* Tears burned the back of her eyes.

"I'm glad he was there to protect you and Jane."

"He was a terrible teaser and a..." Her voice wavered on a teary laugh. "A stubborn old goat."

"I wish I could've gotten to know him better."

She blinked the wetness from her eyes and stared at him in disbelief.

He shrugged one shoulder. "Well, except for the stubbornness and the teasing. Those are horrible traits."

She laughed so long and hard that she had to wipe the tears from her cheeks. She only stopped when she realized Lewis wasn't laughing with her.

He gazed at her as if spellbound. "I love your laugh. I love all of you."

Then why wasn't he sitting on the bed with her? "Are you sure? When people meet me after the show, they often express their everlasting affection. They speak, and sometimes act, without proper thought. That's why I purchased my derringer."

Lewis' fingers curled into fists, like he wanted to punch someone on her behalf. "That's not love."

"Love is complicated. The audience loves what I do, what they see." She shook her head. "But they don't see the real me."

"Because of the layers of your costume?"

"And the layers I've added to hide the past."

"You think I don't see you clearly?"

"You never asked what I did."

"What you did?" Lewis frowned. "What do you mean?"

"When I first met you, I said..." She waited to see if he remembered.

He thought for a long moment and then nodded. "You said, *I'm going to hurt you again*. I still don't understand what you meant. We hadn't really met before. I'd only watched your Medicine Show from a distance. You couldn't have hurt me."

"My show days are over, and this is the truth behind them." She drew in a deep breath and plunged into the unforgiving waters that made up the truth. "Jane always wanted to write and tell you she'd return one day. She didn't want you or her parents to worry. I begged her to wait. I didn't want to risk you finding her and taking her away from me."

"You were young and lonely."

"I was also selfish. I wanted her to stay with me and teach me to ride as well as her."

"I wanted the same."

"You didn't take the one thing that made her happy and make it solely yours. Each day that passed made the letter harder to write, harder to explain why it hadn't been sent sooner. Until Jane decided she couldn't send a letter. She had to come back and explain in person. She was planning that trip when the offer to join Roy's troupe arrived and delayed her again. After her injury on the Mississippi, she refused to return or even write a letter. My selfishness destroyed all her dreams of riding and of returning home."

"John was right. We are all responsible for our own actions. Him and Calhoun. Me and you. And Jane, too." Lewis' brow puckered. "We've all been selfish at some time. Jane wanted to be a star. I bet she stole your limelight when she first joined your show. She wouldn't have been able to resist. I'm sorry."

"Don't be. I wasn't. I needed Jane more than the lime-light. I knew I could do anything if she led the way. I tried to learn on my own, but success always eluded me. I should've tried harder—for Jane and my father."

"You loved them and they loved you back. And not because of what you could do in a show. Love is the greatest thing you could give them. And your love was plain to see and hear, on both sides, especially when your father called you Peanut."

"He said peanuts kept a show alive; despite their size, they made a show thrive." Her throat grew tight. "But when he needed me most, I rode away with you."

"I wondered why you did."

"I couldn't imagine spending another day of my life without you."

A look of wonder raised his brows. "What about the show? What about riding every day?"

"I've ridden every day since I met you."

"Yes, you have." He grinned. "And there are many horses waiting for you to ride at the homestead." His smile vanished, and he muttered a sharp curse. "I'd forgotten about training them. I'll never have them ready in time for the Rangers' return."

"Alone you won't." She leaned toward him, wanting to touch him, wanting him to touch her. "But together we will. Together we are invincible."

He didn't move except to frown again. "You won't miss your audiences?"

"When I'm with you, they fade to a foggy memory. My thoughts are bright with other things. I think about seeing you smile, hearing your laugh, watching you—" She dropped her gaze as she felt her face burn with desire.

"Watching me what?"

She shook her head.

"No secrets, remember."

She raised her chin and said in a rush, "Watching you dive into your bedroll. Naked."

The trunk creaked as he shoved forward to sit on its edge. His gaze locked with hers. "Angel Eyes...will you stay with me tonight? In this room, in my arms, naked together?"

She drew her braid over her shoulder and stood to turn her back to him. "Can you help me undo the buttons?"

With an agonizingly careful slowness, his warm fingers unfastened the first button at the nape of her neck. An instant later, the heat of his lips brushed the same spot. She arched back against him, craving more. He didn't disappoint her. His fingers flew down her spine, opening the buttons as his mouth moved just as swiftly over her neck, her ear, her cheek.

She spun around so he could claim her lips. His possession began slow and gentle, enveloping her in a heady haze of desire that rapidly swelled until his urgency matched hers. Without breaking their kiss, she helped him push her dress off her shoulders, down her arms, and over her hips—to fall in a puddle around her feet. Her undergarments dropped even more quickly, baring all of her to his touch.

He leaned his forehead against hers and broke their kiss. "I'm not sure I can do this as slowly as I want. I'm desperate to touch all of you."

"Noah and Sadie left us water and towels."

"You want me to bathe you again?"

"I want you to touch all of me."

"Once I start, I won't be able to stop."

"Then maybe we'd better bathe each other at the same time. Why don't you remove your trousers and boots while I pour the water?" When she did and turned back to him with a wet cloth for each of them, all of him stood ready for her.

He slid the washcloth over every inch of her skin, following with his lips, soft kisses, little nips, a smile always curving his lips. She did the same. Until she could bear his tantalizing caresses no longer. She took the cloth from him and threw it along with hers into the washbasin. Then she pulled him toward the bed.

As she did, he ran his gaze over her from head to foot. A

wicked grin curved his lips. "You still have your boots on, you know."

"I'll join you on the bed as soon as I can get them off."

He sat down so fast that he bounced on the mattress. A grimace of pain twisted his face, but didn't stop him from pulling her toward him.

"Your back. Maybe we should wait till—"

"We most definitely should not wait." Despite his words, he paused to study her with a long, appreciative look. "But finding the right...position from this point forward might be tricky."

"I excel at tricky maneuvers." She yanked her boots off and put a knee on the mattress on either side of his hips so she straddled him and his erection. The hot, hard length of him rubbing against the sensitive skin of her inner thigh, and higher, made her tremble.

"Easy there, Angel Eyes." He ran his palms over her hips in long, soothing strokes. "I've got you. I won't let you fall."

"But you must." She arched her back to guide him into position. "I have to fall before you can make me fly."

His hands tightened on her hips before returning to their gentle stroking. "Then take the leap—onto me—but only when you're ready."

"You'll catch me?"

"I already have. I can't let you go."

"Good. There's only one direction I wish to go." She pressed down to take him deep inside her, along with an exquisite rush of pleasure. She rose swiftly on another wave just as sweet, eager to take the leap—and the fall—again and again.

He urged her on with the rocking of his hips, the stroke of his hands, and best of all the curve of his smile against her mouth as he kissed her. Over and over. Until her pleasure tightened deep inside and sent her soaring higher than she'd ever imagined possible. Not even in her dreams.

Lewis came with her, surging into her one last time to fly and fall together. He cradled her close as he rolled them both onto their sides to collapse on the mattress. The soft stroke of his fingers on her cheek, her hair, the curve of her shoulder and her hip—brought her back to the present, the chill of the room touching everything he didn't.

When she sat up to pull the quilt over them, his hand ran down the length of her long braid and then, as she lay back down beside him, slid up her spine to cradle the back of her head.

"I can't get enough of touching you," he whispered against her hair as he drew her close again. "Wild horses couldn't drag me away from you."

She snuggled into his embrace, taking care not to touch his bandages. "They will every morning after we return to the cabin."

"But first, I'll get to hold you all night and dream of how I'll wake you in the morning. I have several tricky maneuvers of my own I'd like to show you."

She smiled and laid her ear against his chest so she could listen to the steady beat of his heart as he finally relaxed. "Does Juniper Flats have a minister?"

"It does." His voice grew fainter, swirling around her like a soft cloud promising only fair weather ahead. "It also has a church big enough to invite all of our friends and family to our wedding."

"Then it's not such a bad town after all." With so many blessings, she should be holding a winning hand. But she wasn't. Not with a true evil still prowling the wild Texas land she now loved almost as much as the man who'd fallen asleep holding her.

Wild horses couldn't drag them apart for long, but Wardell could. And before she and Lewis could journey to Juniper Flats' church or even to their cabin, they needed to scour the hills for a man she'd never met but who'd murdered her father and wouldn't hesitate to destroy everything else that she loved.

# CHAPTER 13

Standing in the kitchen, helping Sadie pack provisions in saddlebags, Eldora paused to listen. The house, including Lewis' room, remained quiet.

Sadie didn't stop her packing. "We'll leave as soon as the sun's up, and Lewis and Noah rise with it."

"I wish Lewis could sleep longer. He could use more rest." Eldora couldn't stop herself from gazing longingly at the door to his room.

"Going anywhere near the man you love while he's in bed leads to the temptation to lie down beside him." A smile curved Sadie's lips. "Then neither of you gets any sleep."

Eldora smiled as well. "Did you learn that in Dodge?" She stiffened and added quickly, "In the saloon where you met Noah." She didn't want Sadie to think she'd meant in the brothel Lewis had mentioned.

"I learned many things in Dodge, but never what one assumes a woman alone and down on her luck might discover in such a lawless place. I learned how to love one man and love him well. I also learned how to distract myself with a worthwhile task so I wouldn't make myself crazy thinking about him." She peered out of the kitchen window and sighed. "That hasn't happened in a while."

"What?" Eldora strained to see at Sadie's shoulder and out the window. All she saw was the gloom before dawn reflected in the glass.

"Noah's cattle have broken my garden fence again." Sadie crossed to the mantel and grabbed her rifle before heading to the front door to claim a jacket from a row of pegs.

Eldora followed her. "Where are you going?"

"To fix that fence." Sadie's chin rose to a determined angle. "I want to get as much done as possible so I don't delay our leaving."

Eldora cast a worried glance at the kitchen window.

"I refuse to allow my home to become a prison. I had enough fetters in Dodge to last a lifetime." Sadie squeezed her hand reassuringly. "I won't be gone long. If Noah wakes, tell him I'm just outside."

Eldora retrieved Lewis' revolver and gun belt from the table. "You'll be back quicker if I go with you."

"Now you're talking. Work done with a partner goes twice as fast and is ten times more enjoyable. You'll need a jacket. Wear mine." Sadie tossed her the jacket she'd been about to don and reached for a large sheepskin coat similar to the one Lewis had loaned Eldora.

When Sadie noticed her studying the coat, she ran a reverent hand down the garment. "This is Noah's. I wore it in Dodge. I'm always eager to find an opportunity to wear it again." She grinned at Eldora as they put on their coats. "Since Noah's asleep and you need my jacket, I've decided this is my chance."

Eldora nodded. She looked forward to retrieving Lewis'

coat from the show where she'd left it when she changed into her costume.

With one hand holding her rifle and the other on the door latch, Sadie waited for Eldora to buckle Lewis' revolver belt over her jacket. When they stepped out onto the porch, Eldora scanned the yard for trouble in the form of man or beast. After the recent storms, the early morning hush made the Ballantyne Ranch appear as serene as a pastoral painting, with daybreak teasing the horizon.

Nothing warranted the drawing of her revolver. She kept her hand on it just in case.

As they walked around the side of the house, the hard-packed earth dotted with clumps of brown winter grass gave way to a patch of spring green behind a sturdy fence.

Eldora gasped in amazement. "Your garden's thriving despite your water shortage. How?"

Sadie gestured to the house. "My rainwater collection project."

A network of troughs and pipes snaked down from the roof to several chest-high barrels set at intervals along the wall.

"Even the bunkhouse and barn have barrels. As soon as they're full, we swap them with empty ones and bring the water here. We don't lose a drop."

"Why do you have fences around the barrels as well as the garden?"

"To keep Noah's cattle away. I'm territorial about anything to do with my garden," Sadie said in a firm voice that suddenly softened. "Noah learned that the hard way, but he's grown to love my garden for the bounty it provides."

Eldora suspected Noah most loved keeping his wife happy.

When they reached the break in the fence, many hoof-prints marked the dirt.

"You were right," Eldora said.

"I was wrong." Sadie pulled her down to crouch by the prints. "These tracks look...odd. Too uniform. One doesn't live surrounded by cattle and not notice such things. Noah told me how rustlers used to strap contraptions bearing two hooves in a row under their boots to hide their own footprints."

"You think it's a ruse to draw us out of the house?" Eldora asked.

Sadie crawled close enough to peek around the corner post of the garden fence. She bolted back so fast that she landed on her bottom. She also yanked her rifle up to her shoulder.

Eldora drew her revolver and aimed it at the corner of the fence, and whatever might be coming around it. When nothing did, she whispered, "What did you see?"

"Someone hiding behind the last barrel along the house." Sadie's voice was hushed with dread.

"Who?"

"I don't know. I only saw his top hat."

Eldora frowned. *A top hat? In Texas?* "Are you sure?"

Sadie's grip on her rifle tightened. "Wardell wore a similar hat in Dodge."

"Whoever he is, he knows we're here. He would've seen us come out of the house. What's he waiting for?"

"Maybe for Noah or Lewis to come out as well. So he can shoot them." With her rifle still pointed toward the threat, Sadie glanced over her shoulder at Eldora. "Stay here. I know a path that will take me up behind him. Keep watch in case—"

"No." Eldora winced at the force of her reply and

continued in a low rush. "Remember what you said last night. We stick together."

With a heavy sigh, Sadie nodded and ran in a half-crouch away from the house along the garden fence. Eldora followed her until they halted by the yellow-flowered bushes that formed a u-shaped windbreak around the garden and house. They'd provide the perfect cover to sneak up on Wardell.

Behind them, the house stood half-hidden by the garden. Noah and Lewis were still safe inside. If they woke up, they wouldn't stay inside. They wouldn't be safe much longer.

"Ready?" Sadie whispered.

When Eldora nodded, they crept single file, Sadie first and Eldora following, through a gap in the bushes and down a shadowy footpath. They hadn't gone far when a twig snapped behind them. Eldora glanced over her shoulder and froze.

A stoop-shouldered man in a torn and travel-stained greatcoat aimed a pair of expensive but equally soiled revolvers at them. "Don't turn around anymore than you have, and keep your weapons pointed forward," he said. "Or better yet, toss them on the ground."

"You look like hell, Wardell." Sadie's words shot out, hard and clear, without a speck of fear. "I see Texas isn't treating you any better than Dodge did."

Eldora drew strength from her new friend's bravado.

Wardell snorted a laugh. "I've missed that sharp tongue of yours, Miss Sadie, but my affection for you won't stop me from hurting your new friend. Drop your weapons, or I'll shoot Mrs. Calhoun."

"You won't." Eldora shifted sideways so she stood squarely between Sadie and Wardell, in case she was wrong and he fired a shot and hit Sadie by mistake. "You need me alive to get the Dority land."

"Forgive me for not being precise. When I shoot you, Mrs. Calhoun, it will be to inflict the pain required for you to obey my orders...or maybe so you'll scream for help. If your men come running after you, I will happily shoot to kill."

"I'll scratch your eyes out with my bare hands," Sadie growled, "before I let you do that."

"It's good to see your spirited temperament hasn't been dulled by the dreary routine of a marriage bed. I've waited too long to have the pleasure of bending you to my will." Wardell released a frustrated breath. "I've also spent too long trying to catch your friend in the hills, Mrs. Calhoun. I almost succeeded at the shack before you showed up. For a cripple, the bitch is annoyingly hard to corner. I'm done chasing her around this godforsaken country. With you in my grasp, she will now come to me."

Eldora racked her brain for a way to stall him, to keep him near the house. If she could, Lewis or Noah might sneak up behind Wardell and bash him in the head with a rifle butt.

Wardell surged forward to stand behind her. The barrel of his revolver gouged her cheek while the unmistakably sharp tip of a knife pricked her neck.

"I really don't need you," Wardell whispered close to her ear. "Not beyond tonight. So, if you don't want to bleed out from an assortment of wounds before the sun rises tomorrow, you'll do exactly what I say." He raised his voice so Sadie would clearly hear the rest. "Drop your guns and continue down this path until you reach the barn. We can't walk where I'm taking you. At least not fast enough for my liking."

～

Lewis drifted in and out of sleep, dreaming about Eldora, about living with her in the Dority cabin as husband and wife.

A thunderous pounding, like a fist on wood, made him lurch upright. Alone. Alone in the bed he'd fallen asleep in while holding Eldora. She wasn't anywhere in the room. He rolled off the mattress, gritting his teeth against the pain that stabbed his back. He wrapped the quilt around his naked hips and staggered to the bedroom door.

The pounding came again. Not on the door in front of him, but somewhere on the other side. He wrenched the door open at the same time someone shouted, "Mr. Ballantyne!"

Noah was already sprinting across the room, carrying his rifle and wearing only his trousers. Lewis grabbed his own rifle from where he'd propped it against the wall after he'd followed Eldora into the room. With his hip braced against the doorjamb, he took aim at the front door.

Noah paused to peer out the same window he'd used during his showdown with John, then he yanked open the door. "Clyde, what's wrong?"

The wiry old cowboy pulled off his hat and clutched it in both hands. "Zeke rode in saying he saw Mrs. Ballantyne and another woman riding double on a big black horse. A man was with them. The two horses weren't being ridden hard, but the man's mount appeared tired."

"What'd the man look like?" Noah's question sliced the air like a whip.

Clyde shrugged. "Too far to see."

"Where were they headed?"

"Toward town." Clyde twisted his hat like he might tear

it in half. "I'm sorry. I was keeping watch, but I didn't see Mrs. Ballantyne leave. I—"

Noah clasped his shoulder. "You did nothing wrong, Clyde, but we need to go after them fast. Will you saddle my horse?"

"Mine as well," Lewis shouted.

Noah's gaze cut to him. "You well enough to ride?"

"I'm not staying behind."

"That doesn't answer my question."

"You're wasting precious time asking questions," Lewis growled. "I'm not staying behind, no matter what."

Clyde slammed his hat back onto his head. "Zeke's already saddling Pepper. I'll get your horse as well, Mr. Adams." As he spun away from the door, he called, "We'll have them ready by the time you both get dressed."

Noah hurried back into his room. Lewis did the same. When they met fully clothed in the main room, Noah had also slung a belt of cartridges across his chest. He held another one out to Lewis.

When he grabbed it, Noah didn't let go.

"When we find them," Noah's grip on the belt tightened, "I get to shoot Wardell. Agreed?"

"Agreed."

Noah released the belt and strode toward the door.

Lewis followed close on his heels. "We don't know for certain if the man's Wardell."

"Who else would take Sadie? He's always wanted her. Now he's got your lady, too."

The chill morning air gusting around the porch made him shiver. So did the thought of Sadie and Eldora in Wardell's hands. "He wants our land. They'll be safe until he gets it." Or so he hoped.

Clyde jogged toward them, leading Pepper and Lila, saddled and ready to ride.

"How many came in from the roundup?" Noah asked as he leapt onto Pepper's saddle.

Lewis mounted Lila at a slightly slower pace, gritting his teeth against his body's complaints the entire way.

"Only Zeke," Clyde replied.

Noah reached down and clasped Clyde's shoulder again. "Jacob's still sleeping inside the house. I need you and Zeke to stay with him."

Clyde nodded solemnly. "What if—" He gulped and bowed his head.

"We don't return?" Noah stared at the house, most likely thinking of Jacob losing his parents—much too young, like Noah and his brother had lost theirs. When he spoke again, his voice rasped with pain and regret. "Take him to the Adams Ranch."

"We'll be back," Lewis reassured both Noah and Clyde. "But we can't say when, so take Jacob to my sisters if you need help." With a tap of his heels, he urged Lila into a lope around the western side of the house and its windbreak of elbow bush.

Noah and his gray followed them. "Where are you going?"

"I'm circling around to find their tracks and follow them."

"We don't need tracks." Noah's horse drew even with Lila. "Clyde and Zeke said they were headed for town."

"What if they change course?"

"What if they don't? The *quickest* way to find them is to ride straight for town."

"But the only *sure* way to find them is to follow their tracks."

"Good thing there are two of us." Noah halted his horse.

Lewis reined Lila to a stop as well, so they could finish their conversation head-on. "We can be quick and sure if we split up."

"If by some crazy chance you see Wardell before I do, don't wait for me. Shoot him."

Lewis gave him a mock salute. "Will do."

Noah muttered a curse. "You look pale enough to join the Reaper's next harvest. You gonna be all right on your own?"

"I'll be fine." He searched for a way to make light of his poor health. Noah needed to concentrate on helping Sadie and Eldora, not himself. "It's you I'm worried about. When you get to town, you might run into John."

Noah grunted. "If I do, I'll ask for his help. Who'll help you?"

# CHAPTER 14

*R*iding bareback on Samson with her skirt pushed up over her knees and her hands tied behind her back, Eldora moved her fingers, fighting alternating numbness and stabbing pricks of pain. When the time came to run or fight, she'd need all of her strength.

Silent and stiff, Sadie sat in front of her, her dress hiked just as high, but her hands tied in front so she could clutch Samson's mane.

If Eldora had been alone on Samson, she'd have urged him into a sprint and taken her chances. Wardell must have guessed that. That's why he'd put both of them on one horse and tied them in different ways. He didn't want Sadie to fall off. But he didn't care if both Sadie and Eldora were exhausted by the time they reached their destination, which, judging by their southerly direction, was town.

A lone rider appeared on the horizon. The second one they'd seen since Wardell abducted them.

Like the previous time, Wardell cocked his revolver and kept it low against his body, so the rider wouldn't see its silhouette or its metal glinting in the sunlight. A light gradually fading behind thickening clouds.

"Don't try anything," Wardell said, "or the rider, or one of you, gets a bullet. Hell, I'll probably end up shooting all three of you. But the rider gets the kill shot."

The rider came no closer. He headed in the direction they'd come from and disappeared into the gloom. The wind picked up, and the sky darkened, but unlike yesterday, the rain didn't come.

When Eldora looked over her shoulder, Wardell held a map as well as his gun. He glanced from it to the countryside. Noah and Lewis would need no map. They knew this land. It was their home. They'd follow their tracks or head straight to town. They'd find them.

The only question was would they reach them in time? The wind increased, and Eldora's hopes plummeted. The strong gusts obliterated their tracks. When the evil wind whipped the dirt into their faces, however, it presented the perfect opportunity for a covert conversation.

Before Eldora could speak, Sadie tipped her head down and sideways, as if seeking shelter from the storm in the curve of her own shoulder. "Without the tracks," she whispered, "Noah and Lewis won't be able to follow us."

Eldora strove to keep her voice firm as well as low. "They'll find us in town."

With a final consult of his map, Wardell thrust it in his pocket and herded Samson sharply to the north.

Eldora leaned closer to Sadie and asked, "We've left Ballantyne land, haven't we?"

Sadie gave the barest of nods. "How did you know?"

"Wardell's changed his mind and his heading. Have you been to the Dority homestead?"

"Always wanted to. Having a child left me short of time."

"He's taking us there."

"Then that's where we'll fight him. Tell me about the cabin. What's inside it? Around it?" A gust of grit-laden wind made Sadie cough before she continued in a voice breathless with hope. "Tell me everything. In little bits so Wardell won't notice and get suspicious. We need a plan."

Lewis' words flashed in her mind: *Another revolver and rifle under the bed...enough bullets to stop a hundred mountain lions or heartless husbands and their men. You'll be safe until...*

Until he got home. All of Lewis' plans, and hers as well, had gone off the rails. She prayed her next one wouldn't.

THE DORITY CABIN had never looked so good, standing strong and steadfast—and full of weapons—before them as the wind, and now rain, whipped Sadie's unbound hair and Eldora's braid around their huddled bodies on Samson.

"Remember," Eldora whispered against Sadie's ear. "We move as one until you're inside. Then you leave me and run."

"There must be another way." Sadie's voice had lost its eager edge. "A way where we can stick together."

"No matter what happens at the door, you must reach the bed." Their roles had been set from the moment Wardell tied Sadie's hands in the front and Eldora's in the back.

Only Sadie could aim a gun.

Samson shied away from Wardell as he yanked Sadie off him. Eldora jumped with her, pretending to fall beside her. All the time, she kept twisting her hands, but her bonds remained inescapable.

Wardell hauled them to their feet and shoved them

toward the cabin. Eldora went first. Sadie followed close, clutching Eldora's hands, trying to untie them to increase Eldora's chances of surviving what came next.

There wasn't enough time. They had only one option. Sadie must reach the guns inside the cabin, or they'd both suffer.

Wardell opened the door and pushed them forward again. Eldora staggered inside, then sideways, moving out of Sadie's way, giving her a clear path to race for the bed and its guns. Sadie didn't. She kept tugging on Eldora's bonds. Eldora caught her fingers and squeezed hard. Sadie squeezed back and finally let go—their prearranged signal.

Eldora lurched back against the door and Wardell on the other side. He howled in pain. His arm, caught in the gap, flailed wildly. The door bucked against her as Sadie's footsteps crossed the room.

Eldora pressed her shoulder against the door, dug in her heels, and prayed for the strength to give Sadie enough time. Every second counted.

Wardell groped blindly along the door. His fingers brushed her shoulder, then jerked back. A deafening blast splintered a hole in the wood and exploded in her arm. Wardell had shot her through the door. Shock made her stagger. Wardell's shove on the other side of the door knocked her off her feet.

She put all of her effort into twisting free of her bonds. Only instinct and a lifetime of practice sent her rolling and muted the force of impact when she hit the floor. Nothing could stop the throbbing in her arm. Lightheaded and bleary-eyed, she came to a stop next to Sadie.

Crouched by the bed, Sadie stared, wide-eyed and unblinking, at the door as if lost in a nightmare. The door clicked closed with an unnatural softness, muting the storm outside but not Wardell's heavy breathing inside.

"You won't escape me." He spoke quickly, reveling in his certainty and excitement. "Not like last time."

Sadie didn't move. Eldora mimicked her stillness, twisting only her hands concealed behind her back. She hoped it wasn't the growing numbness bedeviling her body and brain that made her hope her bonds felt looser.

"Lewis and Noah will be here soon," she told Sadie.

Wardell's footsteps came closer. "Not soon enough. And you know it. That's why you're both cowering before me."

Sadie surged to her feet. Whatever had paralyzed her had vanished. The silver barrel of a revolver flashed in her hands. A gunshot echoed in the cabin. Behind Wardell, and slightly to his left, the door splintered again. Sadie had missed shooting him by a hand's-breadth.

Wardell charged forward. He slammed into Sadie, thrusting her hands and the gun up over her head, propelling her off her feet. Sadie hit the wall. Shoulders first. Head next. She crumpled limp as a rag doll onto the mattress.

The gun clattered on the floor. As Eldora rolled toward it, her hands slipped free of the rope. The muzzle of another gun gouged her temple. She went dead still again.

Stabbing pain tormented her hands and arms as her numbness retreated, reminding her that she was far from dead. "You can't kill me. Not if you want the Dority land and its water."

"Your husband believed you were Jane Dority. I'm not so certain. I need you or your friend Dory. Either one of you can pose as the inheritor of the land. I'm wondering if your friend might be more manageable." Wardell grabbed her braid and yanked her onto her feet. His breath puffed hot and fast against her ear. "Calhoun let you rise too high in his show. I'm going to enjoy making you obey my every command. If you don't, I'll bury you deep in the ground." He shoved her toward the door. "Open it."

She complied, eager to get him away from Sadie. Outside, the rain fell in torrents, making it hard to see beyond even the fire pit.

Wardell pushed her onto her knees in the doorway and yelled, "Dory Gypson! I know you're out there. I believe there's also a chance your true name is Jane Dority. Time to do more than watch. Join us, or your friend suffers." He tapped the barrel of his gun against her bullet wound.

Her breath hissed between her teeth before she clenched them against giving him the satisfaction of a louder reaction. "You've lost your mind. Dory isn't here."

"I saw her up by the shack."

"That's miles away."

"She's here. I can feel it."

He'd truly gone crazy. "I saw her in Juniper Flats yesterday," Eldora lied. "She said she was returning to New York. She's far away."

"On the contrary, she's very close. Wherever I've been on this hill, I've felt her watching me. But I seldom see her. For a woman with a conspicuous limp, she's absurdly good at staying out of sight. You'll help me fix that." His gun settled against her wound and did not retreat.

She swallowed her scream.

"Call out to her for help."

"Never."

"You're nothing more than bait. Accept it, and your pain stops." He pressed harder, poking the muzzle into her torn flesh.

Only the chill, wet wind gusting against her face kept her from passing out.

His revolver delved deeper. "Obey me or I'll give you another bullet."

"Go to hell."

Wardell cocked his revolver, and she braced for its retort.

Instead, Wardell yelled, "Your friend whimpers in pain. She's begging me to end her life. What shall I do?"

At the corner of the cabin, a ghostly silhouette appeared and said, "Go to hell."

Wardell flinched and hissed in surprise.

Jane's long braid blew straight as a flag over her shoulder. "Sorry, did you say something?"

He cleared his throat angrily. "I said your friend has been begging me to—"

"She told you to go to hell. So did I. You haven't been listening." Jane limped toward them, revealing her unremarkable but much-loved face. "I've missed your stubbornness, Doro. I wish it hadn't made you leave me."

"Friendship will be your downfall." Wardell's revolver swung toward Jane.

When Jane ducked and lunged forward under Wardell's gun, Eldora jumped up from her knees. They came together, grasping Wardell's arm, struggling to keep his revolver above their heads.

Wardell released a squeak. His hard hold on Eldora's braid vanished as he let go of her to clutch his privates. He glared straight ahead, through the gap between Eldora and Jane. Sadie stood there. She'd slipped out of the cabin to kick Wardell.

"You bitch," he gasped. "You've bruised my balls again."

Blood dripped from Sadie's scalp to her shoulder. She held the revolver they'd fought so hard to gain inside the cabin, but she'd chosen to kick Wardell instead of using it. "You didn't learn anything in Dodge."

"I learned you haven't got the grit to shoot me." Shoulders hunched and back bent, Wardell released his crotch and lunged at Sadie.

Jane drew her arm back. She struck Wardell with the heel of her palm. Blood spurted from his nose as his head snapped up and back. The rest of him followed, toppling into the cabin. Eldora and Jane released his arm rather than be dragged inside with him.

A shot echoed inside the cabin. His finger had either slipped on the trigger, or he was shooting at them.

Jane seized her hand, and she grabbed Sadie's. They scrambled around the corner of the cabin.

Despite a rocking gait that made her lurch from good leg to braced, Jane surged ahead. She pulled them toward the wall of rock surrounding the homestead. "Hurry," she called over her shoulder in a low voice. "We need to reach the top of this ridge."

"We can't climb those rocks," Sadie whispered, voicing what Eldora was thinking. "What about the trail?"

"Too risky. He'll go there first."

"We're safe as long as we stay together," Eldora reassured Sadie, then said to Jane, "I hope you have an ace up your sleeve."

"I have something better." Jane slipped between two sprawling bushes and up a narrow path concealed by more trees and rock.

Wardell's muffled screams of fury grew louder as he left the cabin.

They labored up the path. Jane first, Eldora next, and Sadie close behind. Eldora kept her injured arm near her body and used her other hand to grasp rocks and branches to pull herself along. Staying on her feet had never been so difficult.

Behind her, Sadie slipped and fell to her knees. Eldora reached back and grabbed her hand. Sadie's skin felt cold and clammy. She shook like one of the branches whipped by the storm above their heads.

"Sorry I'm slowing you down." Sadie's voice was so hushed Eldora had to lean closer to hear her. "Got dizzy and couldn't see the path."

Dripping wet, Jane plopped down beside Eldora. "We can only rest for a moment." She tore a strip of cloth off whatever she wore beneath her jacket and wrapped it around Eldora's arm.

Eldora gritted her teeth against the pain even Jane's careful administrations caused.

"Who's your friend?" Jane asked.

"This is Sadie Ballantyne. Noah's wife."

"Lucky fellow." Jane's grin flashed white in the rain. "Remind me never to get in a fight with you. Nice work back there."

"You too," Sadie said. "You're Jane Dority, aren't you?"

Jane went still before finally nodding. "Yes, I am." She finished tying Eldora's bandages and said, "You're good to go." Then she leaned toward Sadie and studied her head. "You bumped your noggin somewhere along the way."

"In the cabin," Sadie replied.

"Shall I bandage it like Eldora's arm?"

When Sadie nodded, the movement made her grimace.

Eldora ripped a strip off her borrowed dress and helped Jane secure it around Sadie's head. "Now we're both good to go."

"Time to leave then. After Wardell dragged you off Samson, I sent him to the top of this ridge. I can't whistle like Eldora does, so I used hand signals. Samson's waiting to carry you home."

The word *you* made alarm race up Eldora's spine. "He's strong enough to carry the three of us."

"We'll talk more when we reach him." Jane helped Sadie onto her feet and gestured for Eldora to continue up the path. "You go first, and Sadie will follow. I'll be behind her."

Eldora grabbed Jane's arm. "Don't be pigheaded. We—"

"We are all tired, but we must keep going." Jane pulled her close and whispered in her ear, "And I'm the only one who isn't bleeding and on the verge of passing out. Now get moving."

Eldora complied, but couldn't stop glancing back to make sure Jane followed. Her limp became more pronounced, but she matched whatever pace Sadie could muster. When they reached the top, Jane put her arm around Sadie's waist, and Eldora did the same. They walked as one until they reached Samson.

He snorted with delight when he saw them. She felt equally happy to see him, but also anxious about what would happen next. This would be Jane's first time on a horse in ten years. If she got on at all.

"Jane, you should mount first. I'll give you a boost and then Sadie next."

"You know it has to happen the other way. Between the two of us, I'm the only one with two fully functioning arms who can boost both you and Sadie onto Samson." Jane set her shoulder against Samson to take the weight off her leg. She leaned forward and threaded her fingers together to form a step. "Show Sadie how it's done."

Eldora shook her head. "I'm not leaving you behind again."

"Good to hear, because Sadie needs both of us right now.

It's time for another leap of faith. Or has your belief in me been depleted?"

Eldora stepped on Jane's cupped hands and used them as a springboard to leap onto Samson. Sadie followed swiftly, but needed Eldora's help to stay on until she got her arms firmly around Eldora's waist. As soon as she did, Eldora reached down to help Jane up.

Jane took a step back and let her hands drop to her sides.

Eldora kept her hand extended. "I'm not leaving without you."

Behind Jane, snapping branches and hurried steps heralded someone scrambling up the path. From the cursing, it sounded like Wardell.

"I'm not bluffing," Eldora hissed. "Remember the Mississippi."

Jane flinched, and her eyes flared wide.

Eldora reached for her again. "Take my hand and get your stubborn ass on Samson."

Jane blinked. She released a low, uncertain laugh, but her movements were swift and sure. She shifted her weight to her uninjured leg, bent in a half crouch, then leapt forward.

Eldora caught her arm. Sadie did as well. Together they pulled Jane up behind Sadie.

"Hold on to me," Eldora ordered as she pressed Jane's palm against her waist. "With both hands."

As soon as Jane obeyed, Eldora urged Samson into a swift walk.

"Where are you headed?" Jane asked.

"Away from Wardell. Other than that, I have no idea. I've never been on this particular patch of land."

"Follow my directions. I'll tug on either side of your coat when we need to turn. Not much has changed on this hillside since I was young. Except for, of course, the waterways Wardell altered."

Eldora stiffened. "Let's keep well clear of anything to do with water."

"Sounds good."

"How can we?" Sadie asked. "The rain is falling in buckets. Noah always worries about flash floods when it pours this hard."

"Gully washers," Jane muttered. "We're going to get a year's worth of baths today." After her accident, Jane had embraced a humorous tone instead of a soothing one to ease people's worries—or distract them from impending doom.

Eldora glanced over her shoulder, trying to read Jane's expression in the rain. "Can you tell me how to avoid those as well?"

Jane's silence was her only answer. It spoke louder than words.

# CHAPTER 15

With Lila on a short rein, trotting behind him, Lewis ran through a frog-strangler of a rainstorm atop the ridge above the Dority homestead. Coming this way had taken time and been a gamble. He prayed it'd pay off. He also prayed he'd glimpse Samson in the corrals below and, despite it being daylight, a light in the cabin's window—which would mean Eldora and Sadie were inside. They had to be here. This was where the tracks led.

Following Samson and Wardell's horse's hoofprints had been another gamble. So had continuing toward the homestead when the wind picked up and he'd lost their trail. Luckily, he'd run across it again after the rain started falling. The wind still blew, but it couldn't erase tracks sunken deep into the muddy earth.

The ground was a lot less muddy up here on the rocky ridge. It was unmarked except for the tracks he and Lila might be leaving. He didn't look back to see. He squinted down at the cabin, straining to see through the torrential rain falling in the murky morning light. Maybe there was a light in the cabin, and the rain was making it impossible to detect.

He'd have to go down for a closer look.

Before he could, he stumbled over a rock. As he glanced from the cabin to the ground under his feet, a flash of muted red in a world of gray made him halt. Dread made him drop to one knee and lean over the spot for a closer look. Blood. Even diluted with rainwater, it was unmistakable. So was the circular hollow holding it, and the multitude of similar depressions nearby. Horse hoofprints. Big ones. Samson's.

How had he gotten up on this ridge? Was Eldora or Sadie with him? Was one of them bleeding?

He raced forward, following the tracks, slipping and sliding as they went down the ridge. He gritted his teeth against voicing the pain he caused his stab wound.

The muffled sound that had echoed in the trees tops many minutes ago suddenly took on an ominous threat. Had it been shouting? Had it been Eldora and Sadie screaming for help?

Through the rain, he glimpsed a big black horse with an equally large rider. When he squinted hard, he realized the rider wasn't one but three. A trio of women holding each other close. The first woman guided Samson with a sure hand that could only be Eldora's. The one in the middle had red hair. The third had a long braid that swung across her back to the tune of Samson's strides. The braid looked identical to Eldora's.

Eldora's words to Sadie and Noah echoed in his mind. *Look for someone like me. My hair, my size and looks.* They'd found Jane!

A tawny beast with four legs and a hitched gait crept between him and the women. The mountain lion had returned. Drawn by the blood, it stalked his loved ones. He yanked his rifle up to his shoulder, braced it, and took aim. The cat vanished into the underbrush.

He'd lost his shot.

Impatient to reach Samson and his precious cargo, Lewis jumped on Lila. And froze. Where was Wardell? Was the man stalking them as well?

Down the barrel of his rifle, he scanned the trees to his left and then right. Far enough away to have to shout to be heard, a man on a horse held a rifle as well, pointed down the hill toward where the mountain lion had disappeared. Noah's broad-shouldered silhouette atop Pepper's pale gray body was as familiar to Lewis as his own reflection in a pool of water.

With a thrust of his chin, Noah gestured for Lewis to continue on his path while he set forth on his.

Lewis nodded. They'd trap the mountain lion between them and maybe Wardell as well. The possibility of not catching the man made his gut clench. None of them would be safe until Wardell was locked in a jail alongside Calhoun.

AHEAD OF ELDORA, slick with rainwater cascading down his black coat, Samson's ears flicked back—listening to something behind them. Something she couldn't hear, but was nevertheless there. He'd been listening for a while now and was becoming increasingly agitated.

Something followed them, stealing closer, stalking them like prey. They hadn't escaped Wardell under the cover of the rain and trees as they'd hoped.

Jane's hold on Eldora's coat tightened, but she didn't tug on either side, asking her to turn Samson.

"How close is he?" Eldora whispered over her shoulder. "Can you see him?"

"It's not Wardell."

"We did it." Sadie sagged against Eldora's back. Her arms around Eldora's waist loosened as well. "We lost him."

"And gained another foe." Jane's hold on her remained firm. "Remember the note you left at the shack?"

The warning about the mountain lion. A frisson of fear shook her. Beneath her, a twin tremor made Samson's muscles quiver, then stiffen. He was done listening. He was prepared to run. The instant someone asked.

She grabbed Sadie's arm. "Hold on to me as tight as you can. This ride's about to get bumpy. Samson wants to race, and so do I."

"Go!" Jane shouted.

Samson shot forward. Eldora turned him onto the nearest downhill path to help him build speed. Behind them the underbrush crashed, then a snarling cry filled the silence. The mountain lion had made its leap and missed. Two gunshots rang out, almost as one.

"Who's shooting at us?" Sadie yelled.

"Don't look back," Jane shouted. "Keep your eyes on Samson's ears."

Eldora drew strength from Jane's comment. Her friend hadn't ridden in ten years, but she remembered at least one trick for staying on a horse.

Jane and Sadie's hold on Eldora's waist remained tight, but their legs lacked the strength to hold their seat riding bareback down a slippery slope. Only Eldora's legs kept them on as she leaned back like a broncobuster perched on a hurricane. She gritted her teeth against the pain that jolted up her injured arm on every jarring stride.

Ears flat against his head, Samson zigzagged through the

trees, bounding over rocks and sliding through the mud. Suddenly, his ears darted left—toward a chasm rumbling with whitewater near his feet. Eldora tightened her hold. So did Jane and Sadie.

It wasn't enough.

As Samson shied away from the drop-off, Sadie and Jane's momentum hurled them forward. They dragged Eldora with them.

Jane released Eldora with a hard shove that propelled her upright. Sadie stayed with her while Jane plummeted into the abyss. Jane had done what Lewis had when they'd raced from the show tent and he'd been stabbed. When Jane knew she was falling, she'd let go rather than drag her friends down with her.

Ignoring the pain from her bullet wound, Eldora wrapped both of her arms around Samson's neck and pressed her entire left side against his, signaling him to turn around. She'd never given him reason not to trust her command. Instinct combined with routine sent him spinning to stand stock-still, puffing hard and facing uphill.

Above them, Jane clung to the edge of a gulch. The water flowing below her paralyzed them both with fear. A horse plowed through the belly-high creek, heading toward Jane. His rider grabbed her arm and yanked hard. She fell onto the horse like a sack of feed slung over the man's lap.

Eldora's fear swelled along with the rising water as it swept them all by her. The man raised his gloating face to stare up at her.

Wardell had Jane.

Two riders crashed through the trees and down the hill. They thrust their rifles back into their saddle scabbards as Noah's pale horse skidded to a stop beside Samson, and Lewis and Lila whipped by, chasing Jane and Wardell.

Noah scooped Sadie into his arms and hugged her close. "Go after them," he yelled to Eldora. "Lewis needs you. We'll follow as quickly as we can."

When she reached them, Wardell's horse had scrambled out of the creek and now raced neck and neck with Lila. Still lying belly down across Wardell's lap, Jane had wrapped her arms around Lewis' waist as he strove to pull her from Wardell's grasp.

Another creek surged down the hill to trap them between the two rising waterways. Below the galloping horses, they combined to plummet over a ridge.

Lewis snatched both Lila's and Wardell's reins and attempted to slow their descent and keep them from tumbling down the drop.

Grasping Samson's mane above his withers, Eldora urged him to go faster. When he came even with Lila, she clambered up to crouch on his back. Then she released him and hopped sideways to squat on Lila's bouncing rump. She grabbed Lewis' shoulders to steady herself. Using both him and Lila as a springboard, she leapt again.

As she landed to sit behind Wardell, she looped her uninjured arm around his neck. Jane still lay across Wardell's lap, holding on to Lewis while he held on to her. Eldora tightened her arm around Wardell's throat and jerked back with all her weight.

Both horses lurched to a halt that launched their riders over their ears. In a blur of falling bodies, Eldora released Wardell and tried to catch hold of Jane and Lewis instead.

She plunged into frigid water that swallowed her whole. Cold. Blind. And alone. Kicking frantically, she rose beneath a tangle of branches. The current battered her as she fought to hold on to the slick wood one-handed. The icy water numbed her injured arm, rendering it useless. It also squeezed her chest in a vise-grip.

She gasped for air. Couldn't breathe. Her grip came loose.

A hand shot down and seized hers. Crouched atop the branches, Jane struggled to maintain her hold on Eldora's slippery hand and keep her above a river determined to wash her away.

"Lord save me from friends wanting to be fish! Why couldn't you land on this pile of twigs with me rather than diving into the water?" Jane heaved on her arm, trying to lift her enough to grab her coat collar. When she succeeded, she grinned. "I've got you now, my slippery little catfish."

"Where's Lewis?" Eldora asked, breathless and shivering with not only cold but dread.

Jane kept up a steady stream of distracting chatter as she hauled her up through a snarl of branches, tree trunks and roots. "Truth be told, Lewis landed fully on these uprooted trees while I landed half in the water. Wardell was still hanging onto me, threatening to drag me down into the river with him. Lewis stopped him."

Eldora kept her injured arm close to her side to avoid scraping it against the branches. When her foot bumped a sturdy branch, she used it and others to climb upward. Jane didn't stop pulling until Eldora collapsed beside her atop the jumble of trees wedged between the walls of the river. Breathing hard, Eldora searched their makeshift island for Lewis.

"When Lewis yanked Wardell off me," Jane added, "they went downriver together."

Eldora crawled to the edge of the trees and scanned the water racing below them. It dropped over another ridge, leaving her blind to whatever lay at the bottom. She sucked in a lungful of air and screamed loud enough to make her voice bounce off the rock walls. "Lewis!"

"Eldora!" Lewis' cry echoed along with hers.

The relieved smile on Jane's face matched hers.

"Where are you?" Lewis shouted. "Where's Jane?"

"We're sitting together on the brush pile," Jane yelled back. "Have you gotten rid of Wardell?"

"He's on the riverbank opposite me. Are you hurt?"

"We're all right." Eldora examined the walls of the river for an escape route so they'd stay all right. They rose tall and smooth above them.

"We've got a problem," Jane called to Lewis. "We can't climb out of this gully washer."

"I'll pull you out as soon as you—" Lewis' shout ended abruptly.

An unsettling hush descended on them as they waited for him to finish his sentence.

"As soon as you swim downriver toward me, you'll be safe." Lewis' voice was firm but also soothing. "Aim for the left bank. I'll catch you."

Jane's face went pale as she shook her head. The rising water rocked the trees beneath them.

Using her good arm, Eldora snatched Jane's hand. "Don't let go."

Jane clutched her fingers tight and nodded. "Together we'll make a bigger target for Lewis to catch."

A rumbling roar rose behind them. When they glanced back, a wave higher than their heads rushed straight at them. They leapt as one into the river.

The water closed overhead, then crashed down to push them deep. They plummeted into even deeper water. Jane's hand miraculously remained tight around hers. Eldora kicked her legs, straining toward the left bank and what she hoped was the surface. Her head popped above the water. She gasped for air. A wave slapped her face, choking her, shoving her underwater again.

Jane's body jerked away from her as if caught on a hook. Her arm snapped straight. The river pummeled her, rolling first her and then Jane like dice. Jane's grip on her hand slipped, as did hers on Jane...until she grasped only water.

The river had won.

Another hand grabbed hers and yanked her free of the water's clutches. The strength in the hand made her think only of Lewis pulling her close after washing her hair.

She landed hard. Instinct made her roll. She came to a halt on her stomach with her cheek against the blessedly solid and unmoving earth. Her lungs burned as she coughed up water and sucked in air.

On the opposite bank, with a churning whitewater river racing between them, Wardell stood alone. Except for a tawny blur that crept and limped closer to him. Wardell fled into the trees. The mountain lion bounded in after him.

Jane's familiar hand clasped hers. "I'm never going near a river again."

Eldora laughed and winced as her body complained. "Rivers are like falling," she whispered. "They seem inevitable."

Careful not to touch her throbbing arm, the hand that had pulled her out of the water turned her to rest on her back in a cradle of steadfast strength and gentleness. Water dripped onto her face. She blinked up through wet lashes, expecting to see a stormy sky above her.

Instead, Lewis leaned over her, water dripping from his nose, chin, and tangled hair. His eyes were narrowed with concern—but also shone with love—as he gazed down at her.

"Have I ever told you," she said as loud as her aching lungs and throat would allow, "that your eyes— No, not only your eyes. That everything about you is stunning?"

Laughter flowed from his lips as he grinned. "I think your fall, and your swim, stunned you."

She smiled back. "A small price to pay to land in your arms. I'd do it all over again as long as you're there to catch me."

# EPILOGUE

*Three weeks after Eldorado Jane's arrival...*

*E*ldora had won their bet and the land, but Lewis hadn't lost. He'd won the heart of the woman he loved, a real home and the sincere thanks of a troop of Texas Rangers.

Ten well-behaved, calm, and content horses—including a once almost unapproachable Appaloosa Cayuse—trotted out of the big corral, ridden by lawmen whose original mounts trailed behind them on lead ropes. They all went down the trail and out of sight, leaving Lewis equally content and extremely relieved to watch them go.

With Eldora's help, he'd fulfilled his contract. He'd kept his word. The Rangers now had spare horses and wouldn't have to burden a single horse with the extreme distances they needed to cover in the course of their work.

Standing beside him, Eldora stared at the trail long after the horses had departed.

"They'll work hard, but they won't be mistreated," Lewis reassured her. "They've found good homes with those men."

"I know. I could tell by the way they spoke to the horses. Patient and gentle. The same way you talked to the Appaloosa after I first met you. After he wasn't so gentle with you and tossed you over a fence."

"You talk to me in the same tone sometimes," he teased and was rewarded with her smile.

"Only when you worry too much. You've no reason to worry about me now," she said in her best soothing tone. "I'm merely sad to see the horses go."

"Even the Appaloosa?"

"He was my favorite." She nibbled on her lower lip to suppress her laughter.

He tried to hide his amusement as well. And failed. Probably because he hadn't tried very hard. He enjoyed it too much when she teased him back.

Her happiness was the elixir that cured everything.

"That Appaloosa always liked you better than me," he said. "I was glad to let you take over his training and entice him into respectability."

Eldora nodded distractedly as her gaze swept the corrals and the horseshoe of rock sheltering them. "It's quiet, isn't it?"

"Up here in the hills? Yes, very quiet. You don't like it anymore?"

"Oh, I do." She drew in a deep breath and her eyes shone with satisfaction until she looked at the trail again. "I meant that it's quiet with the horses gone."

Only Samson, Lila, the mare and her fast-growing colt remained in the big corral. Delilah was with Jane, who'd said she wanted to try riding again while she stayed in Gypson's caravan near Sadie and Noah's house. Jane was safe from Wardell. She'd chosen the trust fund rather than the Dority land. Even though she had, she said she was happy to be home. But she still longed for the show and wanted to use her trust money to bring it back to life.

Calhoun had hanged himself in the town jail before the law or the reporters could arrive. Deciding their hopes for their back wages had died with him, the performers had taken whatever they could ride, drag, or carry. The greatest Wild West extravaganza in the country had ended, not with a prolonged and noisy scandal in the nation's papers, but with a puff of trail dust leaving a little-known town named Juniper Flats.

Vandrill, to Lewis' astonishment, had claimed Brutus as his earnings and turned the buffalo loose to roam the hills.

Hills that had been searched without success for Wardell's body. Either the mountain lion had stashed his remains, or the man had escaped. John had bet on the latter and raced off with Hawk to intercept Judge Trafford.

Vandrill had left as well, muttering something about meeting his mystery woman again. He looked even more out of sorts than when he'd first mentioned her. If Lewis were a betting man, he would've wagered their reunion wouldn't go well.

But gambling wasn't in his nature, and he had more important things to ponder. Like how long Eldora would wait before she told him her solution for a nearly-empty corral.

Finally, she said, "Sadie mentioned a horse in the next county."

"Noah did as well. A rescue from a work camp."

"If that's the case, there'll be more horses in the area needing gentle hands and safe homes."

Lewis nodded. "It'll require *lots* of riding to fetch them all and bring them here for rehabilitation."

She frowned. "You won't mind leaving home?"

"Not if we do a little racing along the way, and you're always by my side."

"You might grow weary of having me that close."

"Never."

"How can you be certain?" She contemplated him from the corner of her eye. "You've only known me for three weeks."

"I've known you since I was eleven." He assumed a fake frown so she wouldn't see his smile. "So you've decided to stay with me for more than a few weeks?"

She nodded, but went back to looking at the trail. She should be looking at him.

"You plan on staying a couple of months?"

Her teeth found her bottom lip again, holding onto her smile. She shook her head.

"A year?"

Her laughter burst free, and so did his.

She spun away from the trail and gazed up at him with her beloved eyes. "You're as terrible a teaser as you are a liar. You know how long. I've told you every day since we got married." She ran her hand over his hair in a soothing caress.

He tugged gently on her braid and its yellow ribbon. "Why not tell me again?"

"What happens..." She paused to worry her lip again. "If you grow weary of hearing the word?"

*Grow weary?* She'd said those words before.

She needed to hear some words from him as well.

"I never will," he replied, this time pitching his voice low, like a solemn vow, as he leaned down to rest his forehead against hers. "Know this: when you tell me how long you want to stay with me, you make everything beautiful."

Eldora pressed her lips to his and whispered the one

word she could say to make him the happiest man in Texas, New York, and probably every state in between.

Eldorado Jane—his Angel Eyes, his riding partner, his faithful shadow, and now his newlywed wife—wished to stay with him for the same amount of time he planned to stay with her—*forever*.

**Thank you for reading Lewis and Eldora's story!**
If you enjoyed their adventure, I hope you'll write a review on Amazon, BookBub, or Goodreads. Or even all three. Every single review helps. No matter how long or short, they are a heartfelt gift that is sincerely appreciated. Hearing from readers makes my day and keeps me motivated to write my next book.

www.amazon.com/author/jacquinelson
www.bookbub.com/profile/jacqui-nelson
www.goodreads.com/jacquinelson

**Want to travel from Texas to the Oregon Trail?**
Keep reading to see my story inspiration for *Between Home & Heartbreak* and then an excerpt from *Between Heaven & Hell* (Lonesome Hearts, book 1) and more.

Wishing you happy reading,
Jacqui

## STORY INSPIRATION & NOTES

I love spending time pondering names. In *Between Home & Heartbreak*, the spark for the stage name Eldorado Jane came from the desire to have a two-part name like Indiana Jones. One part fancy or unusual, the other common or plain. Jane was a quick choice for a common but still beautiful woman's name.

The name Eldora was an easy pick for a short version of Eldorado. The "Dora" part of Eldora led to Dorothy and the last name Dority as well. Dority was also a pick from the TV series *Deadwood* (a violent but also incredibly fascinating series) in which two of my favorite characters were Al Swearengen and his right-hand man, Dan Dority.

Bringing Eldora and Lewis' different personalities together was great fun—as was researching traveling vaudeville performers. America's most iconic Wild West show, *Buffalo Bill's Wild West,* started in 1883 but it wasn't until 1885 that it featured its two equally large but also opposite personalities: the flamboyant embellisher, impresario Buffalo Bill (William Frederick Cody), and the understated but brilliant sharpshooter, Annie Oakley (Phoebe Ann Mosey). He called her Little Missie. She called him The Colonel.

Edgar Allan Poe's poem *Eldorado* (found in this book's preface) provided inspiration before and during writing. After I thought of Eldora casting a soothing shadow over Lewis (when they first met), I remembered Poe's poem. It seemed only fitting that Lewis would soon see Eldora as not only his Angel Eyes but his faithful shadow.

~ Jacqui

**BETWEEN HEAVEN & HELL - EXCERPT**
Lonesome Hearts Series, Book 1

*On a trail full of danger,*
*will he guide her to heaven or hell?*

Hannah knows one thing the moment she enters Fort
Leavenworth—she's arrived in Hell. But inside is the means
to a new life, a position as a scout on a wagon train bound
for the Western Territories. All she has to do is convince the
wagon master, Paden Callahan, she's the right person for
the job.

After his wife was murdered by the Comanche, Paden let his
work as a Texas Ranger consume him. Now he wants
nothing more than to disappear into the West.
Unfortunately, the one man he can't refuse has asked him to
guide a wagon train full of tenderfoots across thousands of
miles of Indian land. But Paden's greatest challenge turns
out to be Hannah, a woman his heart won't allow him to
ignore even though she was raised by an enemy he hates.

*Kansas—1839*

One minute the men were talking to her papa, the next they
shot him dead.

Barely tall enough to see over the windowsill, nine-year-
old Hannah watched the tattered band of militiamen cele-
brate by riding circles around her family's cabin, whiskey

bottles in one hand, roaring pistols in the other. Their whooping laughter conveyed the pleasure they took in taunting those left alive inside.

Terror kicked Hannah's legs out from under her, leaving her huddled on the dirt floor of her home. She clamped her hands over her ears, tried to shut out the gunshots, the pounding hooves, the jeers and calls for her and her mother to come outside.

But Mama did not heed them. Instead, she crouched beside Hannah and fired her own gun to keep their attackers at bay.

Suddenly, all sound ceased.

Mustering what little courage she had left, Hannah rose on trembling legs to once again peer out the window. The men had stopped circling. Had they grown bored of galloping around in the midday sun amid the clouds of churning dust?

Their sweat-streaked faces were lowered as they stuffed scraps of cloth down the necks of their whiskey bottles. Had they grown tired of drinking, too?

Bright orange flames burst from the bottle tops. Putting heel to horse, the renegade mob rushed the cabin. Hannah jerked back in disbelief. The men tossed their makeshift torches onto the roof and then withdrew to a safe distance, knowing she and her mother were still inside. Mama's rifle had told them so.

Dreading what she might see, Hannah's gaze rose to the ceiling. A slash of red ripped across the wood planks, then another and another, like the eyes of a dozen demons. With a shriek, she flung herself into her mother's outstretched arms. The cabin crackled and hissed. The flames snaked all around her, making her skin hurt like she'd come too near a boiling pot.

A shroud of charcoal covered the sunbeams in her mother's hair, and her voice was hoarse with the same ash that choked Hannah's lungs when she spoke. "Climb out the back window. Run faster than you've ever run. Head for the ravine. Hide under its brambles."

Hannah nodded. Mama always knew what to do. She would save them.

Her mother's cornflower-blue eyes glistened. Her gaze slid slowly over Hannah's face as if memorizing it. Then she blinked and her gaze locked on the window. "I'll keep firing. They won't know you've left. They won't come after you if they think we're still inside."

Hannah hesitated.

"Go on now." Mama's push was gentle, but her tone had turned firm. "I'll come as soon as I can."

Reluctantly, Hannah obeyed. She ran until her lungs ached. When she reached the bramble bushes a hundred yards away, she ignored the thorns that tore her clothing and cut her skin. She crawled under the tangle of twigs until she could go no farther. Lying on her belly with her cheek pressed against the hard earth, she listened to the comforting crack of her mother's rifle.

Soon she'd come out and join her...wouldn't she?

Uncertainty pinned Hannah down. So did the brambles above her. She couldn't breathe. She had to get out. With a gasp, she clawed the dirt, trying to scramble back the way she'd come. Her home burst into a roaring ball of fire. *Mama! You have to come out!*

The cabin buckled in on itself and collapsed.

Clutching her knees to her chest, Hannah let her tears burn her cheeks. The militiamen's yelling faded as they left. They left her with no reason to move or live. She stayed under the brambles and gave in to the sweet oblivion darkening the corners of her vision.

The pounding of hooves startled her awake. She squinted through the twigs. The towering funnel cloud of black smoke had faded to a wisp of a memory. A band of raven-haired riders halted between her and the charred remains of her home. Even though she was embedded deep in her hiding place, one of them turned in her direction. And pointed.

They were Indians! Fear constricted her throat. White men had shot Papa and burned Mama alive. What would these people, who everyone called savages, do to her?

They dug her out. When they reached her, she screamed and fought like an animal. The men drew back as if bewildered by such fierceness in one so small. They didn't go far, though. They formed a circle around her. Dark statues with sharp-cut features, they uttered not a word as the lines of their faces settled into impenetrable granite.

Their silence unnerved her as much as the white militiamen's noise. She darted around her cage, seeking an escape. She found none. Gasping for air, she fell to her knees.

A woman pushed through the wall of bodies holding her captive. Hannah tensed, wanting again to flee. But her legs wouldn't obey. All she could do was stare through stinging eyes.

Tall and straight as any queen, the woman wore no jewels or garments of grandeur. Her mane of glossy black hair was her crown, her simple buckskin dress her mantle. She didn't watch Hannah with the curiosity of a stranger or the calculating look of a superior. Instead, her dark eyes glistened with compassion...with understanding.

Surrounded by a ring of emotionless faces and the stench of her smoldering home, the smallest ember of hope flickered inside Hannah. Acting on instinct, she raced forward, throwing herself into the woman's arms—and into a whole new world.

～

To read more about *Between Heaven & Hell*, visit JacquiNelson.com

Keep reading for another excerpt...

**FOLLOWING FAITH - EXCERPT**
Lonesome Hearts Series, Book 2

*Can a single day together on horseback
change your life forever?*

Labeled a harlot and expelled from a remote logging camp
and her work teaching children, Faith Featherby embarks
on a journey to return a stolen spirit horse to the little girl
whose photograph was hidden in the horse's riding blanket.

Orphaned young and stifled by a lifelong shyness, Faith has
only her education as a schoolmistress and her memories of
her mother's stories. She's not an experienced rider, but a
Medicine Hat horse—alleged to have the sacred power to
protect its rider—might be her best hope for surviving the
wilderness... until an Osage warrior rides out of the mist.

Scarred by a brutal past, the warrior challenges Faith to
follow a new path where belief in yourself and your partner,
be they horse or man, can lead to a triumph of the heart.

*Follow a path. Find a partner. Fight for a future together.*

## CHAPTER 1

*Oregon Territory - Autumn 1852*

"You're relieved from your duties, Miss Featherby." Mr.
Hammond tucked his bearded chin under his sagging

collar, seeking respite from the squalls that tested Timber Creek's logging camp more days than not during Faith Featherby's three years teaching in the wilderness.

Although she habitually shied away from confrontations, this wasn't one she could accept mutely. "For how long? The children need me."

Hovering at the foot of the schoolhouse steps, Hammond's usually kind eyes remained downcast as he stared at Faith—or rather her feet, which were frozen in her bewilderment to the threshold of a structure that doubled as her lodgings.

"Your presence as Timber Creek's schoolmistress is no longer desirable," Hammond replied in a staccato voice, as if reciting from a script. Under eyebrows thick as woolly caterpillars, his eyes darted left then right, toward Mrs. Cain and Mrs. Crisp, who flanked him. "The school committee has voted. You're to leave immediately 'n never return."

An avalanche of fear hit Faith. She clutched the doorframe of the one-room shanty she'd transformed into a safe haven for her students and herself. Becoming a teacher had been her ticket out of the orphanage she'd grown up in. A ticket she'd hoped would lead to a better future.

"I've nowhere to go."

Mrs. Crisp's arctic-blue gaze chilled her to the bone. "You'll find room in a bawdy house."

"Jezebel," Mrs. Cain hissed under her breath.

"Whore of Babylon," Mrs. Crisp added, lightning quick.

A gasp broke from Faith's lips before she could swallow it along with her hurt. From day one, the two women had mistaken her shyness for conceit and never uttered a kind word to her, or about her. But until today, they'd never gone so far as to slander her character.

Hammond raised his palms in a placating manner, but

his gaze dipped even lower, locking on his own feet. "Ladies, please. Ain't no need for name callin'."

Mrs. Crisp sniffed in disdain. "She brought this on herself."

"What do you mean?" Faith slumped against the doorway and struggled to speak over her rising panic. "I've done nothing wrong."

Mrs. Cain's spindly body snapped straight as a pencil while her voice climbed high enough to make even Hammond flinch. "You consider relations outside marriage *nothing*?"

"Who said—?" An appalling notion pierced Faith.

Last week Dan Doolan had been furious when she rejected his overtures of *relations outside marriage*, which he'd proclaimed was her only prospect considering her advancing spinsterhood and lack of social graces. He'd preyed on her weaknesses. She could very well end up in a bawdy house—unable to elude men like Doolan—if she lost this job. She had few savings and no family or friends.

She forced herself to stand tall. "I have never participated in relations of those types."

Hammond's eyebrows bunched together as he frowned at the cut line where the woodsmen, including Doolan, labored unseen but still heard. Their constant chopping and cussing filled the air from sunup to sundown.

"You're sayin' Doolan is lyin'?"

If she did not, she'd be branded a harlot. If she did, Doolan would soon be harassing her for slandering *his* name. "He's... not telling the truth." She cringed at the halting quaver in her voice.

Even though Mrs. Crisp stood below Faith, the woman managed to stare down her nose at her. "Mr. Doolan is a long upstanding member of this community."

"I've lived here as long as he has," Faith protested.

Mrs. Cain crossed her arms. "We know him. We do not know you."

Dan Doolan made himself *known* by intruding into people's lives.

Before Faith could round up the gumption to say so, Mrs. Crisp said, "Pegged her for a sinner from the start."

Mrs. Cain gave a curt nod. "Always suspected she was hiding something."

Faith's crippling shyness had prevented her from connecting with anyone in the camp, except for the children she taught. Children had curious minds. Adults often had theirs locked tight. But Mrs. Cain and Mrs. Crisp were right to sense Faith was hiding something. It just wasn't what they currently believed.

"You'd cast me into the wilderness with the"—she gestured to the circle of trees, the lifeblood of this community, and the unknown beyond—"with the wolves?"

"You'll fit right in with them," Mrs. Crisp replied. "And the savages, too. Only you would adopt a crowbait Indian nag and squander your time nursing it back to health."

"The mare deserved a second chance." The sweet-tempered pinto had been ridden until winded and lame, and then discarded to limp into the camp seeking refuge. "Don't we all?"

Mrs. Cain's exaggerated scoff made her rock like a soaring Ponderosa Pine ready to come crashing down. "Not when our children are involved. Only a dullard such as you would suggest such a thing."

"Always questioned her intelligence."

"Probably lied about her credentials."

"We'll file a complaint so no one ever employs her again."

Mrs. Cain and Crisp's swift exchange left Faith's head spinning.

"No, we won't!" Hammond's voice rose along with his gaze until he finally looked Faith in the eye.

Hope flared in her heart and sprang forth in a grateful smile. He wouldn't let them oust her from her home and livelihood. He'd help her.

He blinked as if dumbfounded, and more than a little bedazzled, by her smile. Hanging onto the suspenders bordering his heart, he burrowed his chin back under his collar. "Miss Featherby, I'm sorry, but the school committee's minds are set." He spun away from Faith and her condemners. Once his feet started moving, he gained speed and didn't stop. "You should get goin' before you make matters worse," he called over his shoulder. "God keep you safe on your journey."

∼

To read more about *Following Faith*,
visit JacquiNelson.com

PRAISE FOR THE LONESOME HEARTS SERIES...

### *Between Heaven & Hell*

"A perfect, steady-paced book with poetic descriptions of romance and easy-to-follow fluidity of Callahan and Hannah's journeys." ~ Chanticleer Book Reviews

"A fire-cracker of a love story with the perfect blend of fascinating characters, intense emotion, historical drama and fast-paced action." ~ Scarlett Penn

"Beautiful writing and flawed characters it was easy to care about. A thoroughly engaging story I enjoyed tremendously." ~ Lark

"An exciting journey filled with perilous adventure, this is an original interesting tale with a woven plot line that comes full circle." ~ InD'tale Magazine

### *Following Faith*

"The first story I'd read by Jacqui Nelson which put her on my watch-out-for-and-read-her-stuff list. Despite the short length, this story packed a big punch." ~ Michelle R.

"So well written and so descriptive, you easily get transported to the old west and are traveling on the trail with Faith and Eagle. A beautiful, sweet, romantic, heartwarming story you won't want to miss." ~ Barb

Jacqui Nelson "has a unique way of drawing the reader back

to the old west with colorful descriptions and characters who leap from the page." ~ Jacquie B.

### *Choosing Bravery*

"Grand adventure. Mystery and excitement." ~ Sandra S.

"Action packed, fabulous setting and two main characters you could really root for" ~ N. Love

"One of those stories that just takes you away to a world of the wild west, filled with adventure, suspense and sweet romance. I couldn't put it down." ~ B

### *Rescuing Raven* - free for my newsletter subscribers

"Grabbed my interest from the first page and did not let go until the end." ~ Babs

"Beautifully written...Don't pass this short story by. You will not be disappointed." ~ Sandy S.

"I loved this short story and you will too." ~ Dorothy R.

Deadwood, Dakota Territory 1876...
*In a gold rush storm, can an unlikely pair rescue each other?*
Raven wants to save one person. Charlie wants to save the
world. Their warring nations thrust them together but duty
pulled them apart—until their paths crossed again in
Deadwood for a fight for love.

EXCERPT
RESCUING RAVEN - CHAPTER 1

Fighting a growing impatience fueled by rage, Charlie
Jennings drew his revolver and urged his horse through the
trees flanking the Deadwood Trail. Below him, an
Appaloosa with the strikingly similar color of his own horse
—white covered from head to hock in chestnut spots—was
rein-tied to the back of a buckboard. If the horse hadn't
caught his attention, he might not have given the transport a
second look.

He might not have seen her.

The wagon rattled forward carrying one silent and seven
grumbling passengers. When a bend in the trail cast the sun
in the eyes of the guards, one riding behind and the other in
front, he charged his spotted mare down onto the road.

Everyone in the wagon, except for the cowering raven-
haired woman, screamed. The driver jerked on the lines.

The horses skidded to a halt. The guards scrambled for their weapons.

The click of his revolver being cocked made them all freeze.

The silence that followed was as heated as the summer sun on his back. The guards glared at him through squinted eyes. He kept his focus on them as well—lined up in a neat row down the barrel of his Colt Peacemaker.

"Jennings," growled the closest man, who went by the name Big Bill. "You shouldn't be here."

"Yeah," hollered Bill's partner, a stranger who resembled a beanpole.

Frontier trails and towns had a way of attracting similarly named men, including the Charlies like him. They also had a fondness for embellishment. The deck was stacked in favor of the rear guard being called Skinny Sam or Loudmouth Pete.

"We heard you were guidin' a miner 'n his four kids, the ones who lost their ma, away from Deadwood." At least Skinny hadn't heard, and used, the double-barreled moniker Charlie had been saddled with since arriving in the Black Hills.

"But you," he shot back, "didn't hear that my job finished ahead of schedule."

"Well," Bill said on a long breath, "ain't that a spot of bad luck."

"Not for one of your passengers." He didn't look her way. He'd already seen enough: a ragtag assortment of women, one hunched with her dark head over her wrists tied to the wagon.

To read the rest of *Rescuing Raven*, visit my website JacquiNelson.com and sign up for my newsletter.

# ALSO BY JACQUI NELSON

≈

To learn more about my books, visit my website

JacquiNelson.com

# ABOUT THE AUTHOR

Fall in love with a new Old West... where the men are steadfast and the women are adventurous. You'll find Wild West scouts, spies, cardsharps, wilderness guides, and trick-riding superstars in my stories. Those are my heroines. Wait till you meet my heroes!

My love for historical romance adventures with grit and passion came from watching Western movies while growing up on a cattle farm in northern Canada. I've been nominated for over 20 awards and won the RWA® Golden Heart® & the Laramie® — but my best reward is hearing from readers who have enjoyed my stories.

Email me at Jacqui@JacquiNelson.com

For updates on giveaways, special events, and more, join my newsletter at JacquiNelson.com